Chocs 'n' Snogs

Trying to tell your best mate that you wanted to be more than just good friends was about the most nerve-racking thing in the world. And he did. Oh boy, he did. Every time he saw Sasha, or thought about her, or dreamed about her, his brains just scrambled into a jabbering, hopeless mess.

He just wanted to tilt her head up to his. He just wanted to lift her chin. He just wanted to brush her lips with his. He just wanted to move closer and closer . . .

But you don't kiss a mate . . .

Or do you . . . ?

J-17

Chocs 'n' Snogs

Just Seventeen

Chocs 'n' Snogs

by Kate Tym ♥ Marilyn Walker ♥
Sarah Harvey ♥ Sarah Rookledge

RED FOX

For Mum and Arn – KT

A Red Fox Book

Published by Random House Children's Books
20 Vauxhall Bridge Road, London SW1V 2SA

A division of Random House UK Ltd
London Melbourne Sydney Auckland
Johannesburg and agencies throughout the world

1 3 5 7 9 10 8 6 4 2

First published in Great Britain by Red Fox 1998

Typeset in Sabon by
Palimpsest Book Production Limited,
Polmont, Stirlingshire
Printed and bound in Great Britain by
Cox & Wyman Ltd, Reading, Berkshire

Papers used by Random House UK Limited are natural,
recyclable products made from wood grown in sustainable
forests. The manufacturing processes conform to the
environmental regulations of the country of origin.

RANDOM HOUSE UK Limited Reg. No. 954009

ISBN 0 09 926374 2

Wedding Wobbler

Kate Tym

Matrimonial Torture

'And from our super-deluxe range,' the smooth voice oozed silkily from the television screen, 'the Silver Shadow: who could dream of a more luxurious way to arrive at the church on that most *special* day of your life . . .'

Charley shifted uncomfortably in her seat. The hairs on her arms had started to stand on end, a sure indication that things were getting seriously cringey.

'The proud father of the bride helps his lovely daughter out of the richly furnished interior of the wedding car, her silk and brocade train trailing behind her . . .'

Oh God, Charley thought to herself. She could

1

feel yet another wedding-preparation-induced coma coming on. 'Er, would anyone like a drink?' she said tentatively. Anything to escape from the matrimonial torture chamber.

Her sister Tanya and her soppy fiancé, George, shook their heads slowly, too transfixed by the images of 'the most perfect wedding day ever', even to speak.

'Shush Charlotte, dear,' her mother said. Charley couldn't believe it. Her mother's voice was trembly with emotion. She was watching a promotional video about wedding cars and was already practically in tears! What was wrong with the woman? The whole family, bar her dad and the dog, had gone wedding bonkers. For the first time in about twelve years, Charley was seriously considering running away from home.

She could still remember the day it all started. Soppy George, who had always been a bit of a prat in Charley's opinion, had confirmed it by asking Tanya to marry him. Tanya! Tanya of all people! He could have picked anyone on the planet, three billion people of marriageable age, and he picked Tanya. He was a very sick man.

It was awful. She'd walked into the living room after a day out shopping with Ness, to find her mum crying into a champagne glass, her dad half-cut and looking like he was going to burst with pride, and George and Tanya wrapped round each other on the sofa in a hazy glow of sublime happiness. Then, they'd broken the fateful news to her. Not only had George gone insane and popped the question, but they'd already set the date: Valentine's Day. Soppy George had just managed his soppiest manoeuvre ever. He was at the pinnacle of his career as a hopeless romantic and everyone was going to get to know about it. From that moment forth, Charley's world had started falling apart around her. Wedding mania had hit the Metcalfe family and you either went along with it or got killed in the ensuing crush.

'Er,' she tried again. 'I've just got to pop round to Ness's for something . . .'

'Oh, but Charlotte,' her mum said, genuinely concerned. 'You won't get to see the full range. There are only about eight more to go—'

EIGHT MORE!

'Oh really,' Charley said, trying to sound gutted. 'Oh well, that's a shame. You'll have to tell me all about them when I get back,' she finished quickly, rising out of her seat.

'It's OK, Charley.' Soppy George alert! 'I don't need to return the video for a few more days yet, so you can watch it at your leisure.'

LEISURE! Was he mad? Watching epic videos about leather upholstery and centimetre-wide ribbon bands was not, Charley thought vehemently, number one on her list of top leisure pursuits.

'Yeah, right. Thanks George,' she managed.

'Hey any time,' George winked. 'Anything for my little sister-in-law to be, eh?'

Charley smiled weakly. I'm going to have to kill him, she thought to herself, her teeth gritted. That was George's favourite phrase at the moment. Apparently Tanya thought it was really sweet. Boy did they deserve each other!

Charley lay back on Ness's bed and sighed. 'So then he says, "Anything for my little sister-in-law to be . . ."' She put on a pathetic whingey voice. 'Honestly, Ness, I don't think I can take much more, they're driving me nuts. Even Dad's making himself scarce: I caught him in the shed the other day polishing his spanners. I ask you!'

'Ahhh, well I think it's sweet,' Ness said.

'Sweet!? It's disgusting. It's like they've had a matching set of lobotomies.'

'Oooh, we are bitter,' Ness chided.

'No I'm not,' Charley retorted. 'It's just, who wants to get married these days anyway? It's so outdated. Why can't they just live together? And on Valentine's Day! It's ridiculous – they've picked the most out moded day of the year to do the most out moded thing possible. I mean, honestly, Valentine's Day is so commercial now anyway, if it wasn't for Tanya's wedding, I for one would be boycotting it completely.'

'Ahhh, I see,' Ness said, nodding her head sagely. 'This wouldn't have anything to do with a certain Adam Gerrard, would it?'

Charley looked instantly caught out, tried quickly to rearrange her features, and failed. 'I – well, no of course not,' she protested finally. 'Why should it?!'

Ness softened. 'Oh I don't know, Charley, it's just I thought that maybe as you're not going out with him any more—?'

'So?' Charley was definitely on the defensive.

'So last year on Valentine's Day he was all you could talk about, and this year—' She turned her palms upwards and raised her eyebrows.

Charley sighed, defeated. 'Well,' she spoke quietly, 'it hurts, you know.'

'Yeah, mate,' Ness said, 'but you've got to let go, Charley. He's not worth it.'

'I know, I know. It's just, I feel so hurt, I thought he really liked me. All that time we were together. I really thought I was in love. God, I feel so stupid.' They sat in silence for a moment, before Charley continued. 'I saw them, you know, him and that, that . . . that cow, Harriet, I saw them down town. She looked so smug – the cat that got the cream. And he . . .' she paused, 'he had this expression on his face like . . . like he felt sorry for me!' she blurted.

'Oh Charley, I'm sure he didn't—'

'Oh yes he did. He tried not to, but I could see him

looking and thinking, oh poor old Charley, she's still really cut up over me. And the thing is, I was trying to look as if I didn't care, but I did.'

'Yeah, well you shouldn't,' Ness said firmly, determined to lift Charley from her sombre mood. 'He's an idiot. Anyone who'd throw you over for hairy Harriet Newson is seriously stupid. Anyway, you'll find someone much better than him.'

'Yeah, sure, they're really beating a path to my door.'

'Well, think about it, for every Tanya there's a George,' Ness teased.

'God, is that meant to make me feel better? Imagine ending up with someone like him!'

'But it must be nice, though,' Ness said thoughtfully, 'knowing that someone loves you so much they want to spend the rest of their life with you.'

'Nice?! You must be joking. A whole lifetime of listening to Tanya going on and on about what an important client Mr So and So is, and what an amazing function they put on for Mr Incredibly Rich and Famous . . . blah blah blah!'

Ness laughed. 'Yes well, she is a terribly important person in the field of corporate entertainment I believe,' she said in her best snooty voice.

'Whatever the hell that is,' Charley sneered. 'Standing around in a load of tents eating and drinking all day as far as I can make out. And that's the other thing. She's all smug, because she does deals with all these "venues" and so she's getting "very reasonable corporate rates". Honestly, I've heard the speech that many times.'

'And is Soppy George doing the food?' Ness asked.

'Well, some of his minions are. I mean, poor Georgy Porgy can't be expected to get married and cook!'

'He is a bit Georgy Porgy, isn't he?' Ness sniggered. 'He better lose a bit of weight before heading up the aisle. The vicar'll think they're only getting married because George is pregnant.'

They dissolved in laughter. 'Tanya thinks he's cuddly,' Charley said, wiping her eyes. 'You know that's how they met, don't you? He was doing the catering at one of her dos. She went in there to bawl him out over the quality of the nosh and ended up eating out of his hand – literally.'

Ness squealed, 'Oh God. Don't Charley, you're making me feel sick!'

♥

Nice Frock (Not!)

'Charlotte, come on darling, get up. We mustn't be late for the fitting.'

Charley rolled over in bed. She had been in the middle of a really great dream. One in which Adam had turned up on her doorstep with a huge bunch of roses and was begging her forgiveness and telling her what a complete nightmare Harriet had turned out to be. 'I must have been mad,' he'd said. 'How could I ever have thought anyone could compare to you, Charley . . . Will you ever forgive me . . . ?' She pulled the duvet up over her head and marvelled at just how cruel life could be. She was heartbroken with Valentine's Day looming, and instead of being allowed to just ignore the whole sorry day she was being dragged through someone else's romantic marathon. She didn't want anything to do with this or any other wedding for that matter, yet her mother and sister had got together to ensure that there was no escape. What was the big deal? It's meant to be every girl's ambition, she thought sourly to herself. NASA scientist? Prime minister? No thanks, one day looking like a meringue'll be enough for me.

'Charley.' It was Tanya. 'Come on.'

You'd never believe she'd left home, Charley thought grumpily, the amount of time she spends round here. If they're not pouring over chinaware brochures, they're discussing boring seating plans. 'Well you can't sit Aunty Milly next to Uncle Stan.' In her head she mimicked her mother's voice. 'They haven't spoken to each other since that unfortunate incident with the egg whisk in 1972.'

'Charlotte,' it was her mum again. 'I do think that as your sister has been kind enough to make you her chief bridesmaid you could at least get out of bed in time for the fitting, hmm? Now, come on!'

'OK, OK. I'm up.' Charley rolled out of bed. 'Honestly, someone should tell George what he's doing – marrying in to a full-blown Fascist regime . . .' she muttered to herself, slamming the bathroom door behind her.

'Tanya? You *are* joking, aren't you?' Charley looked over at her sister's beaming face. 'Mum, tell her.'

'Oh, girls,' her mum sniffed, 'you all look so . . . so . . . so lovely!' she gushed.

'Stella, surely *you* see sense,' Charley said, exasperation creeping into her voice.

'I don't know what you mean, honey,' Stella, Tanya's best friend and maid of honour said flatly,

'I really think Tanya's choice of bridal helpers' outfits is just dandy.'

Charley gazed speechlessly around the faces of the three other females in the room before her eyes finally returned to the image in the mirror. Her reflection gazed back at her – a large, apricot, amorphous blob with its mouth hanging open.

'Tanya, please,' she begged. 'I look awful. Don't do this to me. I'll just die . . .'

'Oh nonsense, Charlotte.' Her mum took control again. 'You look lovely. Doesn't she?'

'Sure you do,' Stella, who was American, said. 'I mean, I'm wearing it too, honey, and I personally think Tanya has done a really great job of maximising all our positive features.'

'Stella's right, Charlotte,' her mum tried again. 'You may not think so now, but in years to come, you'll look back at pictures and realise just how lovely you looked.'

Lovely! What *was* it with that word. Her mum's vocabulary seemed to decrease alarmingly as the big day approached. The only word she seemed capable of using these days was lovely: 'lovely flowers', 'lovely service', 'lovely dress'. The poor woman was obviously completely blind – Charley had never looked further from lovely in her life. She'd be the laughing stock, she'd never be able to hold her head up in public again. She was going to be forced to walk up the aisle in front of everyone she had ever known in her whole life – including (the true horror of it had just dawned) Adam – looking like an over-whipped bowl of apricot Angel Delight. God, I hate you Tanya, she thought.

She looked over to the changing-room entrance, where Tanya had just disappeared to try on her own dress, and sighed. She knew she wasn't taking this wedding business with the best of grace, but honestly, why did she have to be so *involved*. Wasn't it enough that she just turn up on the day? Did she have to go through every pre-wedding drama and crisis as it emerged – and did she really have to be a bridesmaid?

Her thoughts drifted. She remembered when she'd gone to Adam's cousin's wedding with him. They'd had such a laugh. She'd looked great that day. She'd saved up to buy a really special outfit and had even had her hair cut specially, and it hadn't been wasted. Adam had been really sweet. He'd said she'd been the most beautiful girl there. Unlike this wedding, where she was going to be the biggest geek going.

Tanya emerged resplendent from the changing room. Stella, beaming, walked behind her carrying her train. Charley didn't know whether to laugh or cry. Was her sister serious?

'Well?' Tanya looked like she was going to explode with joy.

'Oh, darling . . .' Her mother looked like she was going to explode with pride.

Wait for it, Charley thought.

'You look lovely.' Her mum wrestled to get some Kleenex out of her bag. 'Oh dear, girls, I *am* sorry, you must think me terribly silly. It's just, oh, look at my little girl, all grown up.'

Oh gag, this was too much.

'Quick, all three of you, get together, I want to take a photo to show your father.'

Charley couldn't believe it. Her mum had brought a *camera* with her to the bridal shop. She'd already taken three rolls of film at the 'engagement announcement'.

'Hey, Tanya, I hope you've got a stack of photo albums on your wedding list. You're going to need them.'

'Say "cheese".'

'Cheeese,' they chorused. Only Charley added a 'y' to the end.

'There is only one good thing that's going to come out of this whole affair,' Charley said to Ness.

They were holed up in her room having escaped a discussion between Tanya and her mum about the varying merits of 'Rod Ritchie's classic disco experience' and 'Tony Monero – a DJ of flair, charisma and charm'.

'What's that, then?' Ness asked.

'The hen night.'

'Oh yeah,' Ness grinned. 'They're usually a right laugh, aren't they? Where you gonna go?'

'Dunno. You could probably come too, though – they're usually a bit of a free-for-all, aren't they . . . ?'

'Yeah, brilliant. We could go to one of those posh places that your sister can get us into. Like that cocktail place she took us to last year.'

'Oh yeah. God, that was a laugh. She can be all right when she wants to be, can't she?'

'Yeah. So, what's the dress like, then?'

'Hers or mine?'

'Both of them.'

'Terrible.'

'Seriously?'

'Seriously. We are talking total sugar-plum overkill. Stella looks like something out of a Texan mother and daughters pageant – she's in her element, I tell you. Tanya's gone for the full-on fairytale look. Honestly, she'll be all right if she falls in the swimming pool at the hotel, her sleeves are that puffy! And it's got this bodice – sweetheart line apparently – that has a frightening effect on her chest. It won't be her eyes George'll be gazing at on the day, I can tell you.'

'Well, at least he'll get to check out the merchandise before the wedding night,' Ness smirked.

'God, Ness, you're terrible,' Charley laughed.

'And what about yours?' Ness asked.

'Oh Ness,' Charley's voice was suddenly serious. 'It's awful. I look horrendous. And, because his mum's my mum's best mate, Adam's going to be there.'

'No,' Ness gasped. 'Unlucky!'

'I know! And he's going to see me in this awful *thing,* looking more disgusting than I've ever looked in my entire life. And he's going to know exactly why he binned me in favour of Harriet the hideous. Because, although she may be a bit of a pig, she could never look as bad as I am going to look. It's like if Tanya ever possessed even an ounce of taste, it has up sticks and left her. Me and Stella are the apricot dream twins. It is *seriously* bad.'

'Oh, come on. I'm sure it's not as horrible as you think. I bet you look great in it.'

'No, Ness, honestly, I don't – I look horrendous, and I'm going to look horrendous on the day. In front of you, in front of Adam, in front of everybody.'

Surprise

When the phone rang, Charley had assumed it would be Ness wanting the latest update on the crazy world of matrimonial mayhem. It was Stella.

'I'll get Tanya,' she said immediately.

'No, no, honey,' Stella burbled excitedly. 'It's you I want.'

Charley's heart sank. 'Oh, OK, what're you after?'

'Well, Charley, as Tanya's best friend and maid of honour, it is obviously down to me to organise her wedding shower. And as such I'm—'

Charley interrupted. 'Her what? Her wedding *what?*'

'Wedding shower, dear.'

'What,' Charley said, feeling vaguely worried, 'is that?'

'Well now, you know when someone gets married . . .'

'Oh yes, I know all about that.'

'Well, you know the guy has a stag night.'

'Yup.'

'Well, the girl has a shower.'

'Ohh,' the penny dropped. 'You mean Tanya's *hen night*. Yeah, I'd been meaning to talk to her about that—'

'Oh well you mustn't do that Charley, you don't want to talk to *her* about it, dear. It has to be a surprise.'

'Oh, right, OK. So, what'll we do then?' For the first time since all the mindless preparations had kicked off, Charley could feel herself warming to the topic. She could see it now. Tanya and a few of her friends – plus Charley and as many of her friends as she could muster – in some swank bar in town that Tanya could wangle her way into, sipping cocktails, singing along to the juke box, eyeing up some fit boys. Maybe she'd meet someone really nice for a change. Perhaps nice enough even to invite to the wedding. This was more like it. 'We've got to pick somewhere really good. It's not everyday you get married, is it? We've got to make it really special for Tanya.' God this was great. She could wangle herself a freebie night out and make it seem like she was being the doting little sister at the same time.

'Well, I've thought it all through, and you all can come over to my place. I'll tell Tanya I need to see her about something, OK, and you, your mom, your granny and Sue, Trish and Barbie will all be there beforehand to give Tanya a real sur—'

'Wait a minute!' Charley was surprised by the

vehemence of her retort. 'My *mom* and my granny? Are you serious, Stella?!'

'Well sure, why wouldn't I be? It'll be great.'

'Stella, if I can just stop you there.' This was unbelievable. 'We don't really do it like that in this country. You see, we have this thing, it's called a hen night and er, what you do is, you go out with your mates – er, your mom and granny aren't invited, OK. And er, anyway, you go out with your mates and you have a wild time. It's kind of like your last chance to let your hair down before you become a married woman, you know, sort of like one last fling . . .'

'Look, Charley,' Stella seemed to have run out of patience. 'I know you're not taking this wedding thing too well. I know you feel you're losing your sister.'

'Well, I wouldn't say—'

'But, I am Tanya's best friend, and as such I intend to make this the best time of her life. I want her to be able to look back on it and see that everything was just perfect, and that,' she placed heavy emphasis on the word 'that', 'includes her wedding shower. Now, I've set the date for the eighth, so if you'd just like to get your mom for me, I'll explain it all to her. OK?'

'OK,' Charley replied meekly. What was the point of protesting? In the face of the mighty wedding machinery, she was rendered completely powerless.

Charley and Ness stood in front of an enormous

display of crystal vases in Rutherfords, the largest department store in town. Tanya had her wedding list there.

'It's incredible,' Charley said to Ness. 'The first item on the list, right, is a washing machine!'

'No!' Ness gasped. 'You're joking!'

'Nope,' Charley said, 'I'm not. A washing machine, closely followed by a tumble dryer and a food processor. You know, for those of my relatives who might just have a few hundred quid going spare.'

'So what are *you* going to get her?'

'Dunno. There's hardly anything on the list I can actually afford. And anyway, it's all so soulless. You don't even have to go to the shop: you can just phone up and say, "What's on Tanya Metcalfe's list for this much money?" and they'll say, "Oh, that'll be the electric toaster with adjustable slots, madam", and then you say, "Put my name down beside that then," so that no one else can buy it, and that's it. Gift purchased.'

'Nice,' Ness said sarcastically.

'Yeah, but then, I guess if that's what she wants . . . If I don't get her something off the list, it'll end up at the next car boot sale.'

'What about one of these vases,' Ness ventured, 'they're nice . . .'

'Ness, they're revolting!'

'Yeah, you're right. Look, shall we leave it for now?'

'Yeah.'

'Right then. On to the most important task of the day.'

'What's that, then?' Charley asked.

'Valentine's cards of course! I've got at least three potential love candidates lined up for us!'

'Oh, Ness, no . . . Please . . .'

'Come on, don't be such a party pooper. You've got to send at least one. It's the law.'

As Charley and Ness wandered over to the nearest card shop, Charley could feel her heart sinking. She knew Ness was only trying to help, but it wasn't as easy as that. She couldn't send anyone a card, not even for a joke. There was only one boy she wanted to send a card to, and he had a new girl for Valentine's Day, all of his own.

♥

Fun, Fun, Fun!

Charley had had to get to Stella's at about four in the afternoon to 'help blow up the balloons'.

'It'll be a riot!' Stella had enthused. A riot was about the *last* thing it was going to be.

Charley thought she was going to die of embarrassment every time Stella opened her mouth. Didn't she know how cringey she sounded? 'So, Charley,' she burbled. 'Isn't this nice? All the girls together. We really haven't had much time to get to know each other in the past have we?'

Why would we want to, Charley wondered. You're an idiot and I'm not – what more is there to know?

'This is so exciting,' Stella continued regardless. 'I remember when Dave and I got married, we were back in the States then. Well, my best friend Terri-Jo, she threw me the best shower. All my girlfriends were there, it was just great. We did all the traditional stuff. I had to make a hat out of all the ribbons and bows and things that had come off the gifts, and I had to wear it all night! It was so funny – oh, I just had the best time.'

'I can imagine,' Charley said flatly. 'Sounds great!' It was going to be one fun evening.

'Surprise!'

Tanya stood, framed in the doorway, a shocked expression on her face.

'Oh, Stella, you . . . you . . . you shouldn't have.'

No, you're right, Charley thought. She shouldn't have – but she did!

'Come on in, come on in! Now, I'll put the kettle on and then we can really party!'

The kettle, eh? Steady on, Stella, Charley thought sarcastically. We don't want to peak too soon.

Quarter of an hour later, they were all sat around the coffee table in Stella's living room, tea and cake balanced in their hands as Stella started on her first speech of the evening. 'Now I'd just like to take a moment to share with you some thoughts on the nature of marriage. A union of two souls, two hearts beating as one, a love undying . . .'

The hairs on Charley's arms had gone into stand-up overkill. How had her sister ever got hooked up with this flake. Sure, her heart was in the right place, but she was just so . . . weird!

When Charley finally got on the phone to Ness the

next day, she could hardly bear to relate to her the awfulness of the evening before. 'God Ness, it was unbelievable. I actually felt quite sorry for Tanya. I mean, she could have been having a wild night out somewhere in town, when instead she spent one of her last precious nights of freedom stuck in Stella's living room making a hat out of ribbons and wrapping paper! Granny had no idea what was going on and kept asking when Uncle Bob was coming to collect her. Mum kept blubbing. And as for Barbie and Sue – just don't ask! It was hideous.'

'So what did you get her in the end?'

'Well, Stella explained to me how the whole thing about "shower gifts" was that they should be personal and girly, so I got her some knickers.'

'Nice!' Ness scoffed.

'No, they were nice – cream, silky . . . you know, sort of bridal . . .'

'Virginal, you mean!'

'What, for Tanya? You must be joking!'

Charley sat at the kitchen table, her head in her hands. It was getting desperate. Only four more days to blastoff and she still didn't have anything for the happy couple. Her dad came into the kitchen.

'All right, Charley?'

'Yeah.'

'What's up?'

'It's Tanya's present, Dad. I just can't think of anything to get them.'

'What, even with that big list to choose from? You mean you haven't gone for the washing machine!'

'Oh ha, ha. No, you know what it's like, this wedding lark, it's all so prescriptive. It's like, just because everyone else has done it the same way since the dawn of time and asked for the same things and worn the same stuff, Tanya and George have to do it that way as well.'

'But if it makes them happy, love, you should be happy for them too.'

'Yeah, I am. It's just it's all so boring and predict-able, isn't it?'

'You wait till it's your turn: we'll see how you feel about it then.'

'Ha! What makes you so sure there will be a "my turn"? I'm never getting married!'

'Well, we'll see about that. Your mum's started planning it already,' he teased.

Charley smiled. Dad was the only semi-sane one around at the moment.

'Why don't you just get them something off the list,' he continued. 'Something within your price range – like an egg cup!'

'Dad!' Charley laughed. 'This is serious, there's only four days to go!'

'Oh you'll find something, love. And I'm sure, whatever it is, George and Tanya will love it!'

'Yeah,' Charley sighed, unconvinced. 'I suppose you're right!'

♥

Practice Run

'Now, if the bridesmaids could just step to one side at this point.'

Charley gazed at the vicar, nervously. She hadn't been in a church since Adam's cousin's wedding. Churches made her nervous. She and Adam had sat at the back, giggling. They'd really taken the piss out of the bridesmaids' outfits – that'd teach her. Talk about divine retribution. God was certainly getting his own back this time.

'Charlotte,' Tanya's exasperated voice broke through her thoughts. 'Move!' she hissed.

'Oh, sorry. Sorry, your worship.' Charley edged to the side of the aisle. It felt funny going through the motions of the service, in her normal gear. But Tanya had insisted on a rehearsal. That was typical of her, super-double-organised. Whereas, Charley, she'd probably be late for her wedding – not that she was ever going to have one, of course, she reminded herself.

'So,' the vicar continued, 'then we go through the

exchange of vows. Now Tanya, George, did you say that as well as the traditional service vows, you have also written some of your own?'

Charley's hair follicles flickered. No! They hadn't, had they? Blimey, were they gluttons for punishment or what. How absolutely awful. She just didn't want to know what Soppy George was going to vow. 'To warm Tanny-Wanny's slippers every night before beddy-byes.' She snorted out loud.

Everyone, including the vicar, glared at her. He was *really* scary, he looked about a hundred years old and was completely grey: hair, skin, clothes. He looked like a pumice stone.

'Well, we won't go through them now,' the vicar continued, 'as I'm sure you'll want to save them for the day.' Phew! Spared that at least. 'But this is the point in the ceremony where you'll say them to each other . . .'

How long do I have to stand here? Charley wondered. She gazed around the church. It's weird, she thought, I can see why people who've never set foot in a church want to get married in one. It makes it all seem really serious. Like there really is no turning back. Mind you, if you've said 'I do' in here, with that vicar, you'd probably be too scared ever to split up, in case he came gunning for you.

'. . . at which point everyone will be seated and we

will continue with the more general aspect of the ceremony: the hymns, the lesson, the reading . . .'

Yeah, yeah, Charley thought, we get the drift. Can we go now?

'And now,' the vicar intoned finally, 'you may go.'

Thank God – oops, sorry Reverend – thank goodness for that!

♥

The Big Day

On the morning of the big day, the house was in chaos. Charley had never seen so many flowers in her life – their living room was a hayfever sufferer's idea of hell.

Charley had been planning to have a bit of a lie-in. The actual service wasn't until three o'clock and they didn't have to be at the hairdressers until eleven. But, no such luck. Not with Fascist and Fascist Inc in charge of things. Tanya and her mum had been up since five. Her dad had gone to fit in a quick round of golf – 'to calm my nerves' he'd said.

Tanya and her mother had spent the entire morning pacing up and down and shrieking every now and again over something they thought they'd forgotten that they'd actually arranged, provisionally booked, booked and confirmed about eight times in the last six months.

Charley put the telly on. Tanya came in and switched it off.

Charley started making a pot of tea. Her mum came in and took over.

The phone rang. It was Ness.

'So, did you get any?' she asked.

'Any what?' Charley asked, bemused.

'Valentine's cards?!' Ness exclaimed.

Valentine's Day! Ness just didn't give up. With all the fuss over the wedding, Charley had almost completely forgotten that it wasn't only the most romantic day in the world for her sister and George, but that half the nation was simultaneously being swept away in a sea of cards, chocolates and flowers.

'I completely forgot,' Charley admitted. 'I dunno, I don't think so. To be honest, I haven't looked. What's the point. Anyway, there've been so many cards and things through our door this morning, the postman must think we're well fanciable! And, as you know, Vanessa,' she put on a mock-stern voice, 'I really don't care either way. I tell you, this wedding business has put me right off romance! How about you? D'you get any?'

'Yeah, one.'

'Wow! Ex-ci-ting! Who from?'

'My dad,' Ness laughed. 'He sends me one every year. Sweet really . . .'

'Ahh, bless him. Aren't dads great. Mine's getting really wobbly this morning, I can tell you. Every time Tanya walks into the room he has to give her a hug, it's painful.'

'So how's it going? All organised?'

'It's been all organised since about 1986 as far as I can make out, but we still had to get up at five o'clock just to make sure!'

'Ahh, poor you.'

'Yeah, I know. I just can't wait for today to be over . . .'

'Dearly beloved, we are gathered here today . . .'

Charley instantly tuned out and glanced over to the other side of the church. The groom's side. She'd never realised how many relatives George had. There were hundreds of them. Tanya looked pretty unpopular in comparison. Charley had deliberately avoided looking too closely though: she couldn't bear the thought of catching sight of Adam. She felt ridiculous, her dress was puffed, her hair was bouffed and she was wearing so much foundation she felt like her face was caving in. She couldn't believe Tanya had made her do this. As if it wasn't bad enough being dumped by a guy. Did she then have to top it off by having to make a complete fool of herself in front of him.

She tuned back into the vicar's droning voice.

'If there is any impediment why you may not be lawfully joined together in matrimony, you do now confess it or for ever hold your peace . . .'

The church fell into an awkward silence. Oh, here we go, Charley thought. Some wanton Jezebel from

George's past is going to leap up and proclaim him to be the father of her ten kids.

'George Andrew Clavering Scott . . .'

What! What sort of name was that. Oh yes! Charley thought to herself, she could feel years of relentless piss-taking coming on. Clavering Scott! That was priceless.

'Tanya Mabel Metcalfe . . .'

Poor Tanya, she'd always hated her middle name. And who could blame her. But Grandma had insisted, it had been her mother's name and so . . . Thank goodness Tanya had come first. That way Charley hadn't had to be landed with the really crap names. Mind you, Charlotte Ann's bad enough, she thought.

She looked over to where her mum and dad were sitting. Mrs Metcalfe was sniffing into her handkerchief, and her dad, bless him, was holding her mum's hand in his lap. He was looking over raptly at Tanya and George. Every now and then he would turn and look at his wife. Charley felt momentarily moved. They were all right, her family. She was happy for Tanya really. George wasn't such a bad bloke – a bit soppy, but not bad.

'I do,' she heard Tanya say.

'I do,' she heard George say.

Come on, Charley thought, get on with it. She does, he does – what more do we need to know?

'And now,' the vicar spouted, 'George and Tanya

have some personal vows they would like to make to each other.'

'Tanya,' George started. 'You have made my life complete. Without you I am nothing.'

'George,' Tanya took over, 'I can't live, if living is without you.'

What a pair, Charley thought. They were just so corny.

'I know,' George said, 'that there is no one in the world more special than you and I pledge never to forget that and never to let you forget it either. Tanya, I love you with all my heart.'

The church had gone completely silent, as if the entire congregation were holding their breath, as one.

'George,' Tanya whispered, 'I love you with all my heart, too.'

The congregation sighed and Charley, despite her best intentions, felt laughter rising dangerously in her throat. Don't laugh, she told herself, not now. But the more she tried to stifle it, the worse the feeling grew. Oh God, she thought. Think of something boring: maths, physics, geometry. She grimaced in an attempt to squash the giggles that were fighting their way dangerously to the surface, and put her hand firmly over her mouth. Her eyes filled up, with the effort of stopping herself laughing. She tried to get a hold of herself and took a deep breath. Stella, completely misinterpreting the situation, her own eyes brimming with real emotion, leaned over with a tissue. 'Here you go, honey, let it all out . . .'

'You may now kiss the bride,' the vicar said, his tone momentarily light.

George turned and kissed Tanya. Charley's dad turned and kissed her mum. Charley and Stella clutched each other as they sobbed hysterically (for very different reasons) into their Kleenexes.

Disco Fever

♥

'And now, coming at you from the sixties ...' Apparently Rod Ritchie's classic disco experience had won. 'Everybody's favourites, the fab four. Come on grandma, let's see you twist again ...'

'Where did they get *him* from!' Ness gasped. 'He is seriously bad.'

'Yeah, I know, it's like a cheese-fest this whole thing, isn't it?'

'What about the best man's speech? That was something else. Who was he?'

'He's George's pastry chef. Quite cute, isn't he?'

'Not bad looking, but what a loser!' The way he kept saying, "and now this is the really funny part" and laughing, when it wasn't funny at all.'

'God, I know. But my dad's speech was quite sweet.'

'Yeah. "We thought mum had a touch of Spanish tummy and nine months later it turned out to be Tanya" – classic! Hey, and your present, brilliant! What made you think of goldfish?'

'Well, I figured the only thing missing from Tanya and George's build-your-own instant household was a pet. But I knew Tanya would only go for something if it was of the low-maintenance, user-friendly type, so goldfish seemed like the ideal solution. And at least it's a bit more personal.'

'Calling them George and Tanya was really sweet. I guess the fat one's George, then,' Ness laughed.

'Yeah,' Charley agreed, 'and the ugly one's Tanya!'

It was later, when Charley was standing over by the bar, that she finally noticed Adam. Her heart leapt to her throat. He still looked just as good as he always did – cool and confident in a trendy suit. She looked away, scanning desperately for an escape route. I can't talk to him, she thought, I just can't. Not looking like this. I'd rather die, I look so awful. Please, let me off the hook. I can't talk to him now. I need to look fantastic, drop-dead gorgeous when I speak to him, not like this. She glanced over in his direction again. The worst thing she could imagine was happening: he was coming over. The ladies' loo, she thought. If I can just get to the Ladies, he can't follow me in there. I'll stay in there all night if I have to.

'Charlotte, dear, there you are!' Charley's auntie Vi descended on her, a vision in lemon chiffon. 'My dear, you look just dreamy.'

'Thanks Auntie Vi,' Charley said, really meaning

it as she noticed Adam, over her auntie's shoulder, stopping in his tracks and retreating back the way he'd come.

'Your sister's choice of wedding couture has been just sublime.'

'Oh, yes, absolutely.' She tried to re-gather her thoughts and give Auntie Vi her full attention.

'And the ceremony, so moving, don't you think?'

'Mmm, yes.' Charley had now had this conversation about 693 times and it was beginning to wear a bit thin.

Bob, a friend of George's and volunteer wedding video-er, had just appeared and thrust the camera in Charley and Vi's faces.

'Still, I expect you'll be the next Metcalfe girl making a trip up the aisle, eh? You could have your wedding on Valentine's Day, too; that would be nice.'

Charley had finally had enough. 'No it wouldn't, Auntie Vi,' she found herself saying rather more loudly than necessary, 'because I don't recognise Valentine's Day. I don't even have a boyfriend and I'm certainly never getting married!'

'Well, I . . . I . . .' Auntie Vi stammered, for once lost for words.

Bob, who'd been recording the whole sorry business for posterity, turned the camera back on to Charley.

'So, if you'll excuse me . . .' and with a toss of her head she turned on her heel, head down, and marched towards the dance floor. She'd only gone two steps when she walked smack into a large male torso.

'Easy,' a wonderfully rich voice spoke over the top of her head as two strong hands held her steady.

Anger flashed through her, 'Do you mind,' she snapped and she looked up ready to continue her attack. Her jaw dropped open and she stood, idiotically gawping at the most gorgeous boy she'd ever seen in her whole life. 'I . . . I . . .' she tried to speak and failed miserably. The colour rose in her cheeks and all the time his hands continued to burn into her shoulders. He let them drop to his side and Charley felt a tide of disappointment wash over her. Calm down, she told herself. Breathe!

'Um, sorry,' she said, stupidly. 'I didn't see you there.'

'I noticed,' the gorgeous boy laughed.

'Are you one of George's lot?' she asked, congratulating herself on having managed to string one coherent sentence together. God I'm cool, she mocked herself.

'I'm Jake,' the gorgeous boy said. 'George's second cousin, twice removed, type of thing. Y'know what I mean.'

'Oh, right, yeah. You don't look anything like him,' Charley said, 'luckily for you.' She could feel the blush rising again. 'God, sorry, I don't know why I said that.'

Jake laughed, and then they stood in an awkward silence looking at each other. This was too much. Charley stood trapped in Jake's gaze. Neither of them seemed able to break the spell.

'Um, I . . . Would you like to dance?' Jake said suddenly.

Charley thought she was going to faint. Here she was looking like a peach beach ball and this most gorgeous of creatures wanted to dance with her.

'Yes – yeah, sure,' she stammered. 'I'm Charley, by the way, Tanya's sister.'

'I know,' Jake said. 'I asked already.'

Oh my God, Charley thought. He asked already! This was too much.

Rod Ritchie had moved down a gear and was starting to delve into the slow numbers as Jake took Charley's hand and led her on to the dance floor. Charley was in seventh heaven. She hadn't felt this good since . . . She suddenly remembered Adam and glanced quickly around the room to see if she could catch sight of him. Her breath caught in her throat as she finally sought him out – he was standing at the side of the dance floor, a stunned look on his face. Charley felt exhilarated. Ha! she thought to herself triumphantly, see how you like it Adam, as she watched him turn and walk away.

At first she felt awkward with Jake. They had reached the dance floor and started swaying to the music. He kept a tight hold of her hand. She felt strange, light-headed. Whenever she plucked up the courage to sneak a look at him, he was looking right back at her and it was having the most unnerving effect on her. She desperately wanted to put her arms around him and lean her head against him, but she didn't even know him – and he didn't know her.

He was gorgeous, dark brown hair, hazel eyes and full firm lips. Charley shuddered as he took her other hand in his and pulled her towards him. He gently put his hands around her waist; she shivered deliciously and moved her hands around his back. He felt so solid and big under her touch. She leaned her head against his chest and felt his chin nestle gently on top of it. They fitted together perfectly. She couldn't believe it – and on Valentine's Day as well!

When the song finished, they reluctantly pulled apart and walked together to a secluded table in the corner of the room. They sat there for hours talking and talking. Charley felt so comfortable with Jake; it was like she'd known him for years. She could tell him anything. And he was really funny too. She'd been telling him about all the nightmare wedding preparations and he'd really, really laughed. He was just so gorgeous.

At one point Ness had been coming over making a beeline for Charley's table, but when she'd seen

Charley's flashing eyes, she'd taken the hint and done a swift about-turn. She wasn't going to stand in the path of true love, that was for sure.

'So,' Jake asked, 'did you get any valentine's cards then?'

Charley felt herself blushing. 'Er, no . . . I . . .'

'Ahh, you poor little thing,' Jake teased. 'We can't have that now, can we? Let me see what I can do.' He picked a paper napkin up with a flourish and drew a pen from the inside pocket of his jacket. He folded the paper napkin in half and drew a big heart on the front. Then he opened it out and wrote, *To Charlotte, a dream in apricot.*

'Oh very funny . . .' she laughed.

Be my valentine, Love ???

'Here you are then.' He handed her the napkin.

She took it and smiled up at him. God he was a sweetie.

'Well? Will you?'

'Will I what?' she asked coyly.

'Be my valentine?' he asked, leaning so close to her the tips of their noses were nearly together.

'Yes,' she whispered, 'I will.'

Finally their noses touched as Jake leaned closer. Then slowly, very slowly, he moved towards her and their lips met in a wonderful, tingling kiss.

Jake pulled away. 'Happy Valentine's Day,' he smiled.

Mystery Admirer

Marilyn Walker

Welcome To The Real World

Standing outside Josh's bedroom door, Sasha hesitated for a millisecond. She was desperate to tell him her stupendous news, but maybe seven in the morning wasn't the best possible time . . .

Oh, what the hell, she thought, I'm here now. And Josh'll probably thank me for an early morning call – yeah, reckon!

She knocked and charged in, flicked on the light and dumped herself at the foot of the bed. Josh was a good mate, she told herself – the best. He'd understand. And she just had to know more about Greg. Just had to.

'Guess,' she demanded of the snoring shape under the duvet. 'Guess what happened yesterday!'

The snoring halted with a snort. Chestnut hair

surfaced from under the covers, then a pair of blurry green slits and finally a wide sleepy smile. Josh propped himself up unsteadily on one elbow, and squinted with disbelief at Sasha. 'Am I dreaming?' he murmured.

Sasha laughed. 'Wake up Josh,' she said. 'I need some friendly advice.'

He blinked.

'It's so exciting!' Sasha gushed. 'You'll never guess. Not in a million years—' She stopped. His eyes were wide open but fixed oddly on her. She felt about as welcome as a first-date zit.

In fact, all round, she wasn't very popular with anyone in the house at the moment. When Josh's mum had answered the front door, she hadn't even tried to hide her annoyance at being woken up after only four hours' sleep. She kept repeating 'night flight' and 'plane delayed' and 'Austrian air traffic control' like a mantra from some Eastern religion.

Now, gazing down at Josh struggling to wake up, Sasha was certain she'd made a big mistake. Best friends or not, she should have waited until later.

Suddenly, he shook his head. 'Hello, Josh,' he mumbled. 'Have a nice holiday, Josh? It's really great to see you back. How was Austria? Josh, I've really missed you.'

'Sorry,' Sasha pouted, miffed by his teasing. 'I *was* coming to all that. How was the skiing? I like the suntan, by the way. Not mad about the panda eyes, though . . .'

Josh found the corners of his mouth lifting. Sasha's enthusiasm was totally OTT but, as always, he found it frustratingly infectious. 'So,' he said, exhaling deeply. 'What is it I'm supposed to guess?'

'Did you have a good flight back?' Sasha said, turning the teasing back on him. 'How was the snow? More important, how was the après-ski? Don't leave out any juicy bits . . .'

She ducked the pillow that he hurled playfully at her. 'OK, OK, I'll tell you,' she said. 'Who is the single, sexiest, most alluring, most desirable, most wonderful girl in the whole world?'

'No idea,' Josh answered with a sleepy grin.

Sasha batted her eyelashes at him. 'Me, of course! Well, someone thinks so, anyway. Yesterday, while you were yodelling to yaks and shushing down the piste in Austria, we here in Britain were celebrating the quaint old custom called Valentine's Day. And what do you think I got, on that most romantic day of the year?'

'Der,' Josh said, trying to sound even thicker than he felt. 'A valentine's card, maybe . . . Let me guess . . . From a Mystery Admirer? I get it. You want me to do a Sherlock Holmes.'

Sasha grinned wickedly. 'One out of ten for effort. But you're wrong. I know who sent them.'

Josh sat bolt upright. He shook his head to clear it. At the best of times he wasn't the bright-eyed and bushy-tailed sort. After four hours' sleep, he felt more like a sloth on sleeping tablets. '*Them?*'

'Yes, *them*. The biggest, most expensive valentine's card in the whole world, together with the poshest, most expensive box of heart-shaped Belgian chocolates northwest of Brussels . . .'

'Chocolates!'

'Yep. They were far too delicate for a mere mortal postman to heave through our letter box. Some romantic hand lovingly placed them in my porch in the dead of night while yours truly was dutifully putting in a few hours of ridiculously unnecessary beauty sleep.'

'Chocolates! Who sent you chocolates?'

Sasha beamed. 'Greg.'

'Greg! The beanpole!'

'No,' Sasha said witheringly, 'the slim, cute Greg of the gorgeous brown eyes. He sent them. And you know how I like slim blokes.'

'Get with it, Sasha! You can do better than him.'

'Don't be so horrible, Josh. I came here because I needed your help.' Greg's valentine was just about the biggest and most exciting thing that had happened to her for weeks and Josh was being a complete pain. 'Look, Josh, I need to know all about Greg. What does he like? What does he do? Where does he hang out?'

Josh groaned, holding his head in his hands. 'Don't do this to me, Sasha. Not now. I can't take it.'

'But I don't know anything about him. Only that we've been giving each other the eye for a week or two. And whenever I just think about him I go all gooey inside.'

Josh stared down at his hands. Sasha noticed they were trembling. 'This is all wrong,' he said, almost as if speaking to himself. 'It's not a dream; it's a nightmare.'

'Don't be so melodramatic,' Sasha said sternly. 'Honestly, you've only missed a few hours' sleep. Come on, Josh. With friends like you—'

'I'm sorry,' Josh cut in. 'Look, I really am sorry. I think you're making a big mistake, but I'll tell you everything I know about the beanpole. If that's what you really want . . .'

Sasha's eyes narrowed. 'Thank you,' she snapped.

'Welcome back, Josh,' Josh said. 'Welcome to the real world . . .'

♥

Join the Queue

It was twelve thirty. Anxiously, Sasha turned from the clock in the college corridor and for the twentieth time in an hour checked her reflection in the canteen's glass doors. She swung her head from side to side and her honey-blonde hair caressed her shoulders in a satisfying way.

It looked good. So it should – she'd rushed back home from Josh's to dedicate every minute she had to look her best. She worked from top to toe, starting with a full warm-oil treatment for her hair. Then she'd tried on every single thing in her wardrobe at least three times before rashly choosing the red skirt and an even tighter top.

Now, as she turned sideways and checked her reflection again, Sasha knew it was too late to change her outfit. It would have to do. Besides, she didn't want Greg thinking she'd gone to a lot of trouble.

But where was he? She'd been hanging around the corridor for over an hour, waiting to bump into him 'accidentally' on his way into the canteen.

Restless, Sasha turned to look out of the window. Snow had begun to fall. The grey concrete landscape of the college was being lightly dusted with icing sugar. All she needed now was a rug, a roaring log fire, and a warm friendly shoulder – not a million miles from Greg's small but perfectly formed mouth – to snuggle into.

That's if he ever turns up, Sasha moaned. So much for Josh's great suggestion. When he'd grudgingly opened up that morning, Sasha had wheedled out everything he knew about Greg. She'd seen Greg around college, of course. No girl could possibly miss him. He was about ten centimetres taller than anyone else. And he had those scrummy brown eyes like melted chocolate that turned you into a soft centre if they looked anywhere near you. But, despite the fact that they travelled home on the same train, he'd never seemed to notice her.

Until last week.

Judging by his behaviour since then, some strange miracle had turned her into a love goddess. He was always smiling when he passed her. One morning, getting off the train, she'd even thought he was going to kiss her, but he just gave her a soppy lovesick grin. Then, on the morning before Valentine's Day, she noticed that he was carrying a Grisham's bag under his arm. It wasn't until the chocolates arrived, with the valentine that she realised what was in it.

Grisham's was the only shop in their part of town that sold greetings cards and – more importantly – expensive Belgian chocs.

She smiled to herself as she realised what a good detective she'd become. Now all she had to do was to give Greg the chance to admit that he'd sent the card.

She was as nervous as hell. She couldn't afford to get it wrong. Love interest hadn't actually been dominating her life recently. Last term had been all hard work and dull boys. But what was she going to say? Something like, 'Hi Greg, send many good valentine's cards?' or 'Come up and see my Belgian chocolates . . .'?

Sasha sighed. Greg had made it all so difficult. OK, he'd said all those fantastic things in the card about fancying her for ages, and how he was so scared of telling her in case she didn't feel the same. But it would have been so much easier if he'd told her, face to face.

But he hadn't. So here she was waiting in the corridor and anticipating what was going to happen after he told her how he felt. That was the easy bit. Oh yeah . . . She could see it now. She was going to fling her arms around him and give him the most mind-blowing kiss he'd ever had in his entire life. He'd be a quaking wreck by the time she'd finished. Only when he'd recovered would he suggest going somewhere romantic where they could be alone together.

Maybe they'd go for a walk in the park, down by the river. The sky would be blue and cloudless. It would be just cold enough to need to cuddle up together. Not that they'd notice, because they would be wrapped so tightly round each other, their lips would be pressed so close that—

'Hi! Sasha?'

Sasha leaped about three metres in the air. It was Greg! And he was staring at her curiously. Surely he couldn't have read her thoughts. If he had, he wouldn't be standing there looking so relaxed!

She returned to earth on a beetroot-red parachute of embarrassment. 'Hi, Greg,' she muttered, 'fancy bumping into you here . . .'

Greg looked down at her with those big brown eyes, but she didn't melt. She did worse – she froze, speechless.

'Are you going in?' he asked, holding the door.

Sasha told her head to nod but it just jerked a bit as she walked stiffly into the canteen. Pull yourself together you idiot, she warned herself. He's making all the right moves and you're behaving like a gormless kid. Say something for heaven's sake.

'Do you come here often?' she gabbled quickly. 'I mean, to eat. We must be late. It's almost empty.'

Greg's eyes checked out the deserted tables. Apart

from the plump red-faced woman at the self-service counter, they were completely alone.

'Damn,' he said absently.

Not exactly a silver-tongued flatterer, Sasha considered. He hadn't even heard her. As she followed him to the counter she worked out why. He was as nervous as she was, probably much more. He had everything to lose. In the card, he'd laid bare his heart, but he didn't have a clue about how she felt about him. He was obviously waiting for her.

Sasha moved closer to him. Her hand brushed against his as they both reached for the same plate. He smiled sweetly and offered it. Sasha felt her hand tremble slightly as their fingers touched again. When he quickly pulled away, she knew he felt the excitement, too.

As she watched him scooping baked beans on to his plate, Sasha was almost too terrified to speak. She stared absently at a wrinkled sausage, knowing she had to break the silence sooner or later. Poor Greg must have been going through a thousand torments waiting for some kind of sign that she felt the same.

'Did you get any valentines?' she finally blurted out.

Greg shook his head and silently added about a kilo of chips to the beans.

'I did,' she said quietly, wondering how he stayed so slim. 'I got a lovely card and chocolates from someone.'

Greg carefully balanced a fried egg on top of the chips. A single chip toppled off his plate and landed on Sasha's still-empty one.

He turned to look at her and she knew this was the moment she'd been waiting for. He was going to tell her just how much he fancied her. He was going to say that he couldn't sleep at night for thinking about her, that she filled his every thought. Her pulse started fluttering. Her heart was thudding so violently that she could hardly breathe.

Then she realised he was waiting for her to say more. 'Did *you* send any cards?' she asked nervously.

'Course . . .'

Calm now, she told herself. As cool as a canteen chip. This is definitely *the* moment. 'Who to? Anyone special?'

'Someone really nice,' Greg said, licking his fingers. 'Someone not a million miles from this spot.'

Adrenaline surged through Sasha. 'I'm glad you did,' she said, staring dreamily at her plate. 'I've always wanted to tell you, too, but I've never found the—' Sasha broke off, noticing that Greg wasn't next to her any more. He was standing by the cash register. His peepers were out on stalks staring at a tall, willowy girl staggering out of the back kitchen with a huge bowl of soapy water.

Sasha recognised the look on his face. It was the look that she'd hoped he'd be giving *her*. She watched helplessly as the girl ambled casually over to the counter and gave Greg a dazzling smile.

'This is Denise,' Greg told Sasha, his voice deep and lusty. 'Denise started working in the canteen last week. *She's* my valentine.'

Denise looked scathingly down at the single chip on Sasha's plate. 'You on a diet or what?'

♥

Just Good Friends

'You can't blame me,' Josh protested, on their way home from college. 'I didn't know about Denise.'

Sasha sighed. 'It's not your fault,' she said. 'I'm sorry.' Friendship means never having to say you're sorry, she remembered reading somewhere. So how come they'd both been saying sorry to each other so much recently?

She stared out of the train window. The lunch-time romantic snow had already turned to evening slushy sleet. The bleak harshness matched her mood.

'But you did say', Sasha bitched, 'that Greg's always hanging around the canteen.'

Josh took a deep breath. 'But I didn't know why.'

Sasha pulled a face at herself in the window. 'You should have seen him, Josh,' she said with disgust. 'He was like a lovesick puppy. His tongue was practically hanging out. I'm surprised he didn't place precious Denise on top of that mountain of chips and kneel down to worship her. It was cringe-makingly embarrassing.'

'I can imagine,' Josh said sympathetically. 'But I still don't understand why he sent you the chocolates if he's mooning over Dinner-Lady Denise . . .'

Sasha feigned deafness. It was hardly her fault that she'd jumped to the wrong conclusion. All the facts had fitted so perfectly.

'Well?' Josh asked, patiently.

'Look,' Sasha said, irritated, 'I made a mistake, OK. There's no need to rub it in. I've got a Mystery Admirer. I just don't know who he is.'

'You don't know who,' Josh said with a sudden smile. 'There was no name. Greg was just a guess.' The smile died as suddenly as it had arrived.

'Go on, have your bit of fun.'

'You're wrong,' Josh said earnestly. 'I'm not making fun. But, Sasha, you can't go messing about with people's emotions just on a hunch.'

Sasha slumped.

Josh slipped his arm around her shoulder. 'Let's forget all about the chocolates,' he said. 'I'm fed up with them. I can't bear to see you like this. Come over to my place.'

Sasha felt tears welling up in her eyes. Josh was a real mate. He was almost like the sister she'd always wanted – not that he would have been flattered to hear that. She couldn't imagine what life would be like without someone to share the rough and the smooth with. She and Josh had a long history together. They went back all the way to nursery. Their mums had formed a friendship on their very first day. Josh and Sasha had been inseparable from the age of three. They'd gone on to school together when they were five. And until two years ago they'd even gone on holiday to Wales together every summer, staying at Josh's parents' little cottage on the Pembrokeshire coast.

The holidays had stopped when Josh's parents had sold the cottage to pay for a bigger house and moved one stop down the railway line. But she and Josh had still stuck together. It caused a few hassles from time to time when Sasha had to explain to jealous boyfriends that she and Josh were just good friends.

Josh said the same happened to him.

Sasha wondered if Beth was the jealous type. Josh had been seeing quite a bit of Beth in the last few weeks. She seemed nice enough, but Sasha was protective of Josh. He really didn't have a clue about girls, but Sasha wasn't going to tell *him* that. Perhaps Beth would be right for him. He deserved a bit of luck in the romance department.

Me too, Sasha thought, as the train clattered over some frozen points.

'So, who do you think *did* send the card?' Josh asked.

'And the chocs,' Sasha added idly, mentally making a list and crossing off names. It wasn't a very long list: very quickly she reduced it to two.

'Pete must have sent them,' Sasha said mechanically. 'It's obvious. His mum and dad own Grisham's.'

Josh shook his head.

'The card', Sasha explained patiently, 'was delivered by hand, and Pete Grisham knows my address. He used to deliver our paper for his mum and dad's shop. Also Grisham's is the only place that sells those foreign chocs.'

'Let's make sure this time. I'll ask Pete. I don't want you making a fool of yourself again.'

'Thanks,' Sasha said, 'but I won't. Not this time. I was a fool to think of Greg. It has to be Pete. Remember the way Pete behaved at the party last month? He practically stuck to me like glue.'

'He'd had too much to drink.'

'You really know how to give a girl a compliment.'

'I didn't mean it that way. Look, Sasha, I think there's something you should know . . .'

There was a squeal of brakes as the train shuddered to a halt.

'Too late,' Sasha said, grabbing her bag and making a mad dash for the door. 'This is my stop. Wish me luck. I'll give you a ring to let you know how it goes. I just know it's going to work out this time.'

♥

A Glass Wall

Josh forced a smile for Sasha as the train pulled out of the station. Inside, he was furious. He punched the seat.

'I sent the card!' Josh gritted out. 'If Pete hadn't ruined everything with his stupid, stupid chocolates, Sasha would know how I feel about her by now.'

Since Christmas, when she'd playfully kissed him under the mistletoe, Josh had been painfully aware that his feelings for her had swung from friendship into something much deeper. He should have just poured out his heart to her instead of sending a card. He should have told her how things had changed, how he had to be more than just a friend. He should have . . .

But I'm too stupid! he thought angrily.

A week ago, when he'd decided to send the valentine, it had all seemed so easy. He was sure she would be excited at having a Mystery Admirer. And together, according to his plan, they would have solved the mystery . . .

The holiday had been the only problem. His parents had booked the skiing trip months ago. Back last June, no one had noticed. No one had cared – least of all Josh – that the last day in Austria was Valentine's Day.

But he'd found the perfect solution. Beth offered to deliver the card for him.

He'd carefully chosen Sasha's valentine. Mainly blue, because she couldn't stand pink; no slushy message, because she didn't really like commercial sugar and spice – he'd made up his own romantic message to go inside because she loved that sort of thing. Of course he hadn't signed it. Mystery Admirers don't. It had seemed more romantic. And he'd been petrified that Sasha would laugh at him.

Trying to tell your best mate that you wanted to be more than just good friends was about the most nerve-racking thing in the world. And he did. Oh boy, he did. Every time he saw Sasha, or thought about her, or dreamed about her, his brains just scrambled into a jabbering, hopeless mess.

He just wanted to tilt her head up to his. He just wanted to lift her chin. He just wanted to brush her lips with his. He just wanted to move closer and closer . . .

But you don't kiss a mate.

He couldn't bear to lose her. If he made a move and she turned him down . . . If it ended their friendship . . .

It wasn't fair. He could put his arm round her – in a friendly way. He could hold her hand – as a mate. He could kiss her cheek – like a brother. But there was always a wall, a great big three-metre-thick glass wall called friendship, that stopped him going further.

Josh felt physically sick.

What an idiot you are, he thought to himself. She's throwing herself at Pete, and you're sitting here feeling sorry for yourself.

He looked so depressed that a twenty-something couple, cradling a baby between them, looked up from the seat opposite and gave him a pair of sympathetic looks. Even the baby gurgled.

No, Josh thought with finality. No, she's not going out with him! I'm going to stop her.

Something had got to change – and fast. If he had to lose Sasha's friendship, then so be it. But if he didn't even *try* to tell her how he felt, he would never be able to forgive himself. He decided to run all the way back from the next stop to Sasha's house. He would tell her the truth. He would pull her into his arms and say—

'Josh? Is that you? I thought it was . . .'

He flicked his eyes up. Beth was walking down the centre aisle of the carriage. She sat beside him. 'It's happened,' she said, ashen-faced. 'We've split up. It's over.'

An hour later, they were sitting in Beth's kitchen.

Josh had walked her home, and given up all hope of getting back to Sasha before she went out. Instead, he'd found himself playing agony aunt again. It's a cruel joke really when you think about it, he mused. He, who'd never really loved a girl until Sasha, was handing out words of wisdom like he was some kind of expert Romeo.

He didn't fancy Beth, but in the last four weeks they had come to depend on each other. Beth with her boyfriend trouble; Josh with Sasha. It had started one afternoon, when he'd been hanging round the college gates waiting for Sasha. Beth was waiting for someone, too. He'd struck up a conversation about how cold it was, when suddenly she'd burst into tears.

Since then, they'd spent loads of time together discussing the problems of her relationship and the non-starting of his.

'It's definitely over this time,' Beth was saying as she made another coffee. 'Matt doesn't trust me.'

Josh smiled, partly at Beth, and partly at the irony of his situation. The world was standing on its head. Sasha was probably with her Mystery Admirer right now. 'Do you want me to talk to Matt?'

'Please. Just explain that I was buying the chocolates for Sasha. As a present from you.'

Josh's blood iced up.

'I don't want the money for them,' Beth babbled on, 'after all you've done.'

'Beth,' Josh said, slowly. 'What are you saying?'

'I saw the chocs in Grisham's,' she said. 'They looked so romantic. I really wanted someone to be buying them for me. But I couldn't resist. On impulse, I bought them and delivered them to Sasha's with your card. Did she like them?'

Josh gasped.

'Josh! Did I do something wrong?'

For a moment Josh couldn't speak. His mind was doing overtime. *He'd* 'sent' the chocolates. There was no rival Mystery Admirer; never had been. It was all just a misunderstanding.

But Pete *was* real. And very soon Sasha would be in his arms. Josh felt like tearing his own hair out, strand by strand.

He pulled himself together and tried to smile reassuringly at Beth. He took out a tenner. 'If I wasn't such an idiot,' he said, 'I would have thought of the chocolates myself. I've got to call Sasha. I just hope I'm not too late.'

♥

Crossed Lines

Sasha kicked off her shoes and flung herself on to her bed. She felt strangely elated. The last few hours were very nearly a terrible disaster.

She reached for her bedside phone.

Josh took ten seconds to answer. 'Sasha!' he said, delighted. 'At last! I've been trying to reach you all evening.'

'I was down the club with Pete,' Sasha said, surprised at how happy she sounded. 'I had a great time.'

'You sound like you enjoyed yourself,' Josh grumbled.

'Well, you know what a brill dancer Pete is,' Sasha said. 'My feet are killing me.'

'And did you and Pete . . . ? I mean, are you seeing him again?'

'He's a lovely bloke,' Sasha said, plumping up her pillow to make herself more comfortable, 'but he isn't exactly Mastermind, is he?!'

Josh made a sound that was half-cough, half-laugh.

'What did you expect? We're talking about Pete aren't we. He's a nice bloke, but—'

'He's two brain cells short of a pair,' Sasha giggled. 'Seriously though, I don't know how I didn't notice until tonight that he was so dumb. I know I've never been alone with him before, but . . .'

'Sasha, before you go on, there's something I'm desperate to tell you.'

'Let me finish first,' Sasha cut in. 'I called round his house about eight and got him to ask me if I wanted to go down the club. He was delighted when I "agreed". He just kept on staring at me like I was Christmas and birthday rolled into one. He didn't say a single word all the way there. At first, I thought he must be wearing a Walkman. Then I decided he must be lethally shy. But anyone who gets out on a dance floor and dances like that . . . Wow! Shy just isn't in it!'

Sasha took a deep breath before going on. 'Honestly Josh, Pete is drop-dead gorgeous, and really quite sweet in his own way, but when it came to handing out brains they must have tripped up and dropped his share into his feet. A gagged clam would be easier to talk to. I swear to God, I counted every word he said. Thirty-five! Thirty-five words all night and thirty of those were "yeah".'

'So why are you so happy?'

'Because, my sweet grumpy friend, he told me he didn't send any valentines this year, which is just as well, cos if he'd had anything to do with it the card would have had no *message* on it, as well as no name. So, naturally I'm delighted, cos if he didn't send it then someone else did.'

Sasha held the phone away from her ear as a strange strangled sound came from Josh's end of the line. 'Are you OK?' she asked. 'Josh?'

Josh's voice was shaky when he replied. 'Look Sasha, I've got something important to tell you. I don't really want to say it on the phone. Can I come over?'

'What is it?' Sasha asked. 'It's very late.'

'I need to tell you face to face.'

'Come on, Josh. Tell me now.'

'No! It's too personal.'

'It's about you and Beth, isn't it?' Sasha probed, her curiosity lifting. What's happened? Tell me.'

'It's not about Beth,' Josh said gently. 'I went to see Matt tonight. I think that's all sorted out now. It's about you.'

Sasha was confused. 'What's Matt got to do with any of this?'

'Forget Matt,' Josh said, exasperated. 'I want to talk about you.'

'You brought Matt up, not me. First you tell me you went to see him, then you won't tell me why. What's going on, Josh?'

'For God's sake, Sasha, will you just shut up and

listen for once. It's nothing to do with Beth or Matt. It's about you.'

Sasha nearly fell off her bed. That didn't sound like a friend. She'd never heard Josh explode like that in all the years she'd known him. Whatever was eating him must be pretty damn serious, but she was exhausted. 'It's too late to come round,' she said. 'Tell me all about it tomorrow.'

'OK,' Josh said, his voice a mixture of excitement and fear. 'I'll be round soon as I wake up.'

As she put down the phone, Sasha racked her brains for anything that could be that important to Josh. And then it struck her. It had to be the valentine's card – Josh must know who sent it.

And who had Josh spoken to tonight? Matt. He said he'd been to see Matt.

Matt!

Yes, that made sense. Matt had always been a bit flirtatious. Their eyes had met and lingered on more than one occasion. But Matt had always been fully booked on the romantic front.

Now she thought about it, whenever she'd seen Matt in the last week, he'd been on his own. So it was Matt. It had to be him. Hey, things are looking up after all.

She grabbed the phone. Josh answered straight away.

'I've got a sneaking suspicion' Sasha taunted, 'that

you know more about the card and chocs than you've been letting on.'

The line crackled and Josh cleared his throat. 'I do,' he said. 'I know who sent them.'

Josh's admission clinched it, Sasha decided. 'Me too,' she gabbled excitedly. 'Oh, Josh, isn't it wonderful? I'm going to ring him now.'

'No!' Josh shouted. 'Listen! There is no him. It's me. *I* sent them!' But he was too late. Sasha had hung up already.

♥

Twelve Hearts That Beat
As One

Sasha snatched up the phone as soon as she'd hung up. Matt was a bit withdrawn but seemed keen to meet up with her. 'I'll bring a video round to your place,' she suggested brightly.

'Great,' Matt sighed. 'See you tomorrow.'

After her parents had left for the supermarket the next day, Sasha was in the bathroom faster than you could say 'Body Shop'. The shower gel, body and facial scrub, revitalising shampoo and conditioner, styling mousse, after-shower body lotion, super-enriched face cream and her fave body spray took a real punishing in the next ninety minutes.

After that, she really got to work in front of her bedroom mirror. It's funny how things work out, she mused, applying lipstick. Matt had been going out with Beth Philips for ages, and now Beth was with Josh. In an hour or so, she and Matt . . .

Sasha slipped into the clinging satin dress she'd selected last night. 'If that doesn't suck your babyblue peepers out of their sockets, Matt,' she said to her reflection in the full-length mirror, 'you have my permission to become a monk.'

Sasha cursed the fact that Josh would be asleep for hours yet. She wanted to know more about Matt. He was in the same year at college, but wasn't in any of her classes. She did know that he was more interested in sport than literature, and was built for speed. He was tall and taut with muscle in all the right places. His tanned skin glowed almost golden and he had shoulder-length curly blond hair that he tied back when he was flying down the wing, playing rugby for the college.

As she picked up the phone, her mind was conjuring up images of Matt's golden arms wrapped tightly round her. It took all her self-control to keep her voice casual. 'I'll pop round, then. No, of course I won't take ages to get ready. I'll be straight over.'

Two hours later, Sasha sat next to him, still waiting for those strong brown arms to reach out for her.

The sci-fi video was playing but neither of them had watched any of it. Sasha had given up when Mordran, a two-headed alien from the papier-mâché planet Tharg, had appeared in the first scene.

Matt hadn't even watched that much. He was staring into space. Exciting or what! Sasha decided to prod him into action. She reached into her bag and pulled out the handmade chocolate hearts. There were twelve of them, nestling under a clear plastic cover and a beautiful silk bow.

She held the box out for Matt to choose, wondering if he would pick the one she would. She felt drawn to one slightly misshapen one in the left corner. It was like an afterthought; it wasn't as perfect as the rest.

Almost without looking, Matt reached down and grabbed three chocolates at once. He absently poured them into his mouth. Three gyrations of his rock-like jaw later, his hand was coming back for more.

'Do you mind if I turn this film off?' Matt asked gently. 'I'm not really in the mood.'

Sasha perked up. At last! She snuggled against his shoulder.

Matt reached for more chocolates. 'It's really nice of you to try cheering me up,' he said, forlornly, 'but I can't stop thinking about Beth. I'm so miserable without her.'

Beth! Sasha shot away from him, stunned. 'Why did you send me a valentine if you're still hung up on Beth?' she demanded indignantly.

'I didn't send you anything,' Matt gulped. 'Why would I? I've got ...' he sighed. 'Rather, I *had*, Beth.'

Sasha could feel the embarrassment spreading up her throat and painting her face. 'Then why did you let me come over here and make a fool of myself?' she snapped angrily.

Matt stared at her like she *was* the two-headed Mordran from Tharg. 'I thought you'd come to cheer me up. I assumed Josh had told you how miserable I was.'

'Josh didn't say anything about it,' Sasha said. 'Matt, what's going on?'

He took a long deep breath. Sasha could almost see his confused thoughts stumbling backwards and forwards like a rugby scrum. Eventually the ball emerged. 'Josh was over here last night,' he explained, munching another chocolate. 'He told me he wanted to make it clear that there'd never been anything going on between him and Beth – just friendship.'

Sasha didn't even try to hide her confusion.

'It's simple,' Matt said. 'Beth bought some chocolates for a valentine present. Only, I bumped into her in Grisham's when she was getting them. She looked dead flustered. I was flattered. I sat back and waited for them to arrive on Valentine's Day. And guess what? Zippo. Zilch! They didn't come. I didn't get the chocolates because she'd got them for someone else. I was furious. And I told her.'

'But what's Josh got to do with all this?'

Matt tried to grin – and failed. 'I didn't know who she'd been two-timing me with until Josh turned up last night. Beth and Josh'd made up some ridiculous rubbish about Josh wanting to send a valentine's card to someone. But, as he was in Austria, Beth was going to deliver it for him in the dead of night.'

Sasha felt a cold tingle of panic creep up her spine.

'As if!' Matt sneered. 'And it gets better. Apparently, Beth decided to buy a box of chocolates and deliver those, too. She thought it was more romantic. What a pack of lies. And do you want to know the best bit? Josh wouldn't even say who he was supposed to have sent the valentine to. They must think I'm thick – expecting me to buy a story like that.'

'I don't think so,' Sasha said, her mind racing ahead. Her heart was pounding, thudding in her ears. She lifted the almost-empty box of chocolates and held it under Matt's nose. 'Were these the chocolates Beth bought?'

Matt stared long and hard as if seeing them for the first time. 'Yeah. They were exactly like that. How on earth did you . . . Oh, no!' he said, realisation breaking across his face. 'You!'

'Beth was telling you the truth,' Sasha said in a tiny voice. 'She *did* deliver them in the dead of night. To me. And that means Josh . . .'

'No wonder she hates me,' Matt groaned.

'What have I done to you, Josh?' Sasha groaned back.

They stared at each other for five long minutes, each locked in their own private hell.

Sasha broke the silence. 'Look, Matt,' she said. 'I've got to go.'

'No!' he pleaded. 'Stay! You've got to help me. I've got to get her back, but what do I do?'

She hardly heard him. One word was repeating over and over in her brain. One name – Josh! Now it all made sense: his odd behaviour, the thing he was going to tell her, her insensitivity. Josh!

In the background, somewhere light years away, she could hear Matt's voice.

'Do you think I should buy Beth something?' he was asking. 'Not chocolates, though . . .'

It was wild and crazy. No wonder she hadn't worked out who'd sent the card. Josh! She wouldn't have guessed in ten million Valentine's Days. Sasha groaned. Josh could have turned up with 'Sasha, will you be my valentine?' tattooed on his forehead in Day-Glo letters and *still* she would have missed it.

'I've got it,' Matt's voice cut back in. 'Listen, Sasha. Sasha?' He shook her gently. 'I'm going to buy the biggest bunch of flowers I can carry, rush round to her place and suggest giving our relationship a second chance. What do you think? You're a girl.'

'Rush round with flowers, yes,' Sasha said, distantly. 'You've almost got it right.'

'And then?' Matt asked desperately.

'Get on your knees and grovel.' Sasha was stuffing her things back in her bag. There was only one chocolate left in the box. She packed it carefully and reached for her coat.

Matt was smiling hopelessly.

Poor Matt, Sasha thought. Physically he was as strong as an ox. But emotionally he was as weak as a kitten. Inside that dense mass of muscle and bone Sasha knew there were twelve hearts: eleven tiny chocolate ones – and one huge, sad broken one.

She had to keep telling herself to stay strong, to stay in control.

'Matt,' she said firmly, 'trust me. It'll work if you love her the way you say you do. Get round to Beth's, and beg forgiveness . . .'

♥

Sharing Is Sweet

Sasha slammed Matt's front door and was showered by a mini-avalanche of snow from the roof of his porch. She didn't care: nothing could dampen her excitement.

Now she knew for sure who'd sent the card and chocs. This time there could be no doubt. It was Josh. He was her Mystery Admirer. He'd got Beth to deliver for him while he was on holiday.

What a blind stupid fool she'd been. All this time she'd been chasing shadows when the truth was right in her face.

Sasha would have blushed if her cheeks hadn't been frozen white by the biting wind and the icy swirl of dusty snow. She was a total idiot. Imagine discussing other blokes with Josh like a complete lovesick girly when all along he was . . .

What must he have been thinking? Oh no. It must have been a real smack in the face:

'Don't you think Greg is just wonderful? Eh, Josh? He's just right for me . . .'

'Pete! He's a great dancer, Josh. Powerful thighs and nice bum . . .'

'You like Matt, too, don't you Josh? Those full lips of his . . .'

No wonder Josh had been acting strangely. Every single thing she'd said to him since he got back had been a huge put-down.

Josh! Poor, sweet, wonderful Josh. Her whole body rippled with goose bumps as she saw him for the first time with new eyes.

As she hurried towards his house, she started to panic. What if all her silliness with the others had put him off? She couldn't bear the idea. All the time they'd spent together, all those years of loving him as a friend, had just been preparation for the real thing. She couldn't lose him now. Not now.

Sasha started to run. By the time she reached his house she was gasping for air.

She felt like she'd been hit by a real avalanche when Josh's mother told her he wasn't in.

'I *have* to find him,' Sasha pleaded. 'Where can he be? Any idea?'

'Sorry,' his mum said, shaking her head. 'Come in and wait, though.'

'Thanks. Can I use your phone?' A few useless phone calls later, Sasha was miserable. No one had seen him. Unless . . .

She picked up on his mother's growing concern.

'Don't worry, I know where he is,' Sasha lied, desperately hoping that her guess was right. She didn't know what she would do if she was wrong. And her recent guesses hadn't exactly been too accurate!

The weather had worsened by the time she stepped back out on to the street. In fact, it was almost a blizzard. She couldn't see more than a few metres.

Almost on autopilot, she turned left. Two hundred metres to Frimley Gardens. Turn right. Down to the shop. Turn left. She knew this journey better than the back of her hand. She must have walked it a thousand times in the last two years.

Normally, it took Sasha ten minutes. But tonight it took a full twenty to slip and stumble home.

Every step, she fought the rising panic. Please, Josh, she prayed, don't let me have spoilt it. Forgive me . . . I know you will.

The darker, uncontrolled parts of her mind tormented her. Of course he won't want you now. He gave you a wonderful valentine's card and you went swanning after three blokes who probably thought you were a complete airhead.

Sasha dragged herself up the pathway leading to her house praying that he'd phoned, praying that someone had been in to take a message, that she'd know where to find him.

She cursed: the door was locked. The house was dark and deserted.

She'd just put her key in the door when a dark shadow moved towards her from the blackness of the garden.

'Sasha, is that you?'

'Josh?'

As she spoke, his face emerged from the shadows. His lips were grey in the dim street light, and his teeth were chattering uncontrollably.

Then he smiled and her insides did a double somersault. She stared up at him and saw his hesitation.

'I know the truth, Josh,' she said gently, taking his frozen hands in hers. 'I know it all now.'

Josh didn't wait for more. His mouth was on hers, urgent, exploring every contour of her lips. Sasha thought she was going to fall, her knees felt so weak. But Josh just held her closer, kissing her more and more passionately. Sasha had never known anything like it in her life.

She was still floating when they pulled apart for breath.

'We've got to go inside, Josh,' she whispered, frightened to break the spell. 'You're frozen.'

'Not any more I'm not,' he grinned, still shivering.

'How long were you waiting?'

'I don't know,' Josh said. 'Ages. I decided I didn't want to waste another minute. I wasn't going to miss you again. I had to tell you. But how did you find out?'

Sasha put a finger across his lips. 'I just know,' she said. 'I guess I've always known; I just didn't want to admit it. I was too afraid to lose my best friend.'

'Never,' Josh said solemnly.

'So what do we do now?' Sasha asked, knowing it was a silly question.

Josh answered as they stepped into the hall: he took her in his arms and kissed her again and again. She never wanted that blissful, shared moment to stop.

When it did, Josh couldn't drag his eyes off her.

Sasha was almost scared by the intensity of his gaze. And her own feelings. Things had happened so fast. Then she remembered it was Josh. Wonderful Josh who knew everything about her, who'd seen her at her best and at her worst, and miraculously still cared.

He cared enough to stand all day in a blizzard just to see her. He cared enough to declare his love in a card and risk her turning him down.

'I haven't thanked you for the card and the chocolates,' she said, guiltily remembering where most of the chocolates were. She took out the box. 'The last one's for you.'

Josh looked at the delicate heart. 'It's yours.'

'No, I want you to have it.'

Josh smiled. Sasha's own heart skipped a beat – how come she hadn't noticed just how beautiful he was?

'Is this our first row?' Josh teased.

Sasha shook her head and lifted the chocolate to

her mouth. Her eyes were challenging and wicked. 'If you won't eat it,' she teased back, 'we'll have to share it.'

She held the tiny heart between her teeth and carefully guided it towards Josh's lips . . .

The Direct Approach

Sarah Harvey

Love Is In The Air

'Love is in the air, everywhere I look around . . .'
Flora bellows loudly and not particularly tunefully
into my ear, as we walk towards the college canteen
together. It's only a week to Valentine's Day, and
she's in the mood for Lurve with a capital L. But then
again, isn't she always? Self-styled queen of hearts,
this is Flora's favourite time of year, where she really
gets to totally overindulge in her ration of passion.
Everybody turns to look at her as she saunters into
the canteen singing like a wailing moggie in the
mating season, flamboyant in hot-pink trousers,
and a little white top. But Flora doesn't care, she
loves to be the centre of attention, almost as much
as she loves to be in 'Love'.

Flora's my best friend. One sixty centimetres, cute and blonde, confidence on legs. Small in stature, big on personality. Once she's set her sights on a guy, there's no stopping her. 'Will you be sending any cards this year, then?' she demands, as we take our place in the queue that's straggling past the trays containing what the college rather libellously calls 'food'.

'Nope,' I state emphatically.

'Why on earth not?' She makes it sound like I've just announced I won't be breathing any more or something – like sending a valentine's card is absolutely vital to life's continuing existence.

'Because there's nobody that I particularly want to send one to, that's why,' I mutter, preparing myself for the usual onslaught.

While I wouldn't mind the odd chance to share some impassioned lip wrestling with a gorgeous morsel of maledom, it's certainly not the only reason I'm on this planet. Unfortunately, Flora just can't understand how I can be happy without having a boy in my life. To her, luscious liaisons, love letters, hot dates and snogfests are the secret to eternal and everlasting happiness.

'There must be somebody,' she says incredulously. 'What about David Cator? Don't you think he's fit?'

'David Cator? He's about as tempting as the food in this canteen,' I giggle, helping myself to a rather suspect-looking burger complete with limp lettuce, and melted cheese not unlike the thick paste they use to stick things in art lessons.

'Sam Rickard, then? He's gorgeous.'

'Sure, undeniably cute, but way out of my league.'

'Jordan Daish? Don't you think he's got one of the best little butts ever to grace a pair of 501s?'

'He's a nice arse, but he's already going out with Hayley Jenkins.'

'Lewis James? Richard Tebbut? Alex Goldman?' she asks hopefully, running out of possible candidates.

'Look Flora, they're all quite nice, but I don't really fancy any of them OK . . . Besides, who's to say any of them would be interested in me?'

Flora crosses her baby blue eyes in despair. 'What am I going to do with you, Sophie?' she sighs. 'You just don't realise what you're missing out on by being so backward in coming forward!'

'What about you? Will you be sending any cards?' I engineer a rapid focus-change from my love life – or rather lack of it – to her own abundant one.

Fortunately this works.

'Will I be sending a valentine's card!' she shrieks. 'Is the food in this place totally inedible? Is getting through all of your meagre clothes allowance before the sales even start bound to happen? Does my little brother have worse table manners than your dog?' I'll take that as a yes, then.

'So who's going to be the lucky recipient *this* year?' I ask her.

As you can probably imagine, Flora is not particularly constant in her affections. She falls in love as regularly and as readily as you or I clean our teeth. Last Valentine's Day she had to write a list to make sure she didn't miss sending a card to any of the guys she fancied, although I must admit that just lately she has managed to get it down to one hot favourite at a time.

'Who do you think!' Flora demands, as though the answer is as obvious as the spot on the end of her nose that she hasn't quite managed to hide with cover-stick. 'Ed, of course!'

Ed Baines. Of course! Thinking about it, she has mentioned him quite a few times recently. In fact she's mentioned him about every six seconds for the past week or so. I should have guessed that he was the object – or should I say sitting target – of her latest infatuation.

She gazes over to where Ed is currently sitting in the corner of the canteen with a bunch of his cronies.

'Isn't he just gorgeous . . .' she sighs happily.

'Yeah, he seems pretty nice.'

'Pretty nice?' Flora explodes, like I've just insulted him. 'That's the understatement of the decade, Sophie. He's a total babe, don't you think?'

'Yeah, sure he is.' I can answer this honestly. Ed *is*

cute, I can see why Flora likes him. Strange though, I wouldn't have thought he'd be her type at all.

Ed's one of the in crowd. He has to be really – he has all the right qualifications, sporty and sexy, clued up and chilled out – but he's slightly different from the others. Flora can be so over-the-top sometimes, and while Ed's a lot of fun he's also pretty quiet really, kind of shy without being shy, if you know what I mean. I suppose he's not quite as loud as the other guys in his group, he's certainly not as loud as Flora!

'Quick!' she shrieks so loudly into my ear that it pops. 'There are some spare spaces at their table, and Rachel Taylor's moving in for the kill.'

Like a madly competitive kid determined to win at musical chairs, Flora chucks our lunch money at the dinner granny on the till, and then thunders down the length of the canteen, food tray in one hand, my wrist clutched firmly in the other, and skid-slides into the orange plastic seat next to Ed, just before Rachel manages to park her bum in it.

I collapse next to her, just about holding on to my lunch tray, which I nearly lost in the wild stampede across the room. Thank goodness I didn't go for the soup! As it is, the top half of my burger bun shot off somewhere in the first few metres, despite the cheese superglue, and my chocolate pud's a quivering collapsed mess on a plate.

'Hiya, Ed.' Flora moves into automatic simper, flirt-to-kill mode, her long mascaraed eyelashes fluttering on overdrive like moths caught under a lampshade. 'Fancy a bite of my hot dog?'

Unfortunately, Rachel Taylor is still glowering above us, hands on hips, scowl on face.

'I was just about to sit there!' she squawks. Rachel, a pouting prima donna, just about stops short of stamping her feet, but she's still pretty close to a temper tantrum.

'It's all right,' Ed smiles, politely declining the chance to share sausage with Flora, and stands up. 'I'm just off to football practice, you can have my seat.'

I don't know who looks more disappointed – Flora or Rachel. They both wanted to sit next to Ed, and now they've ended up sitting next to each other.

Purposely ignoring Rachel, Flora covetously watches Ed and his mates strut across the room, like a hungry dog contemplating a plate full of hot sizzling sausages. At least she's managed to control the drooling.

'Football eh . . . Perhaps we should go and watch a game some time,' she muses thoughtfully. 'It's a well-known fact that, if you want to get to know a boy, then a good way to do it is by taking an interest in his interests.'

'But you hate football.'

'Noooo . . .' she hedges, 'I never said I *hated* football.'

'You said, and I quote, "What's the point of a load of hyperactive blokes running round a field chasing a piece of inflated leather."'

'Well, that was before I really understood the game . . .'

'Don't you mean, that was before you found out that Ed plays?'

'Of course not!' she denies – or should that be lies? – vehemently. 'Football's one of my favourite games. I definitely think we should be out there, cheering our boys on, showing some team spirit.'

'Well, even if you *have* suddenly developed a new-found passion for footie, it doesn't mean *I* want to go out in the middle of winter and stand on a freezing sideline.'

'Pleeeasse Soph,' she pleads. 'Come to the next match with me, it'd look a bit suspicious if I turn up there on my own. I'd do the same for you, you know I would.'

She gives me the puppy-dog-eyes treatment, all sad, and grovelling.

'Pleeeaasseee . . .' The puppy-dog eyes don't seem to be working, so she tries the eyelash fluttering on me instead.

'OK, OK, I'll go with you.' I hold up my hands in submission. 'Anything to stop such a sad exhibition.'

Flora immediately goes back to her usual buoyant self.

'Great! I knew you'd do it. Oooh I could snog you. Nope, I think I'll save that for Ed when our team wins . . . You never know,' she grins wickedly, 'I might just get to swap shirts with him after the match!'

'Couldn't you just stick to swapping telephone numbers like most normal people?' I ask hopefully.

It's nearly six o'clock. It's almost dark. The temperature must be subzero. We've been standing at the edge of the football pitch for nearly an hour. My hands are so cold they feel like a row of frozen fish fingers in the freezer. My toes have all drained of blood, and are curling toward the soles of my feet, trying to hide underneath for warmth, and my ears have turned a rather fetching shade of cobalt blue. To think, I could be at home now, curled up next to a roaring fire, with a mug of steaming cocoa, and a good soap on the TV. Instead I'm stuck on a sports field which is more like an ice rink, waiting for the start of a boring old football match.

'Isn't this great?' enthuses Flora, stamping her feet to bring back the circulation, her breath curling in icy smoky tendrils around her own frosty pink-tinged ears, her heavily mascaraed eyelashes gradually turning white at the ends as though they've been sugar-frosted.

'Sure, if you're a soccer-loving snowman,' I reply dryly. 'Which I'm not.'

'You just wait till all the guys come out in their skimpy little shorts,' she grins. 'Then you won't be complaining. The temperature'll get so high the ice on the pitch will melt!'

'If you say so . . .' I reply, totally cold and unconvinced. 'But can I just ask you one question?'

'Sure, what's that then?'

'When are the boys coming out, and why are we the only ones here?'

'That's two questions,' hedges Flora.

As if in answer to these two simple (yet I feel very relevant) questions, a much-muffled man, who very sensibly appears to be wearing at least three coats and whose head is almost completely swathed in a scarf like a mummified Egyptian, scurries across the field, almost goes straight past us in the gloom, and then, spotting Flora's luminescent jacket, skids to halt a few paces away.

The scarf is lowered, and a pair of watering grey eyes assess us questioningly. It's Mr Mason, the sports coach.

'What on earth are you two doing out here at this time of night?' he barks sharply.

'Just waiting to support our team.' Flora adopts her enthusiastic, good Girl Guide attitude, mainly used in the presence of difficult oldsters.

'But the game's been cancelled due to the bad weather. Don't you girls ever read the notice board?'

He pulls his scarf tighter around his neck, raises his dark shadowed eyes to heaven, and then scurries on to miserably scrape the thick ice from his car windscreen, complaining about winter, and muttering about 'idiot girls' under his breath.

Mum forcibly crowbars the dog from the hearth rug, and then parks us both in front of the fire to defrost.

Gradually my body starts to thaw out, but I still can't help being a bit frosty with Flora.

She always goes so over the top when she decides that she likes somebody, and I'm normally the sad mug that gets dragged into the middle of it all.

'You're mad,' I announce to Flora, once my tongue has unfrozen from the roof of my mouth.

'You what?'

'I've decided that you're completely mad, certifiably insane. You must be: only a crazy person would do what we just did in the hope of bumping into a spunky bloke.'

'Nothing ventured, nothing gained,' grins Flora, totally unrelenting. 'If you want something you just have to go out and get it.'

'Yeah, but when it comes to guys it's not just about you wanting him. It's better to know if he wants you too. I always think that you should leave it to them to make the first move.'

'Oh no. You can't leave it to them! Boys don't know what's good for them,' Flora says wisely. 'Sometimes you just have to steer them in the right direction. Trust me. Ed wants me. He may not know it yet, but he wants me.'

'OK if you say so,' I grumble, finally feeling warm enough to take off my coat and gloves. 'Just don't try and include me in any more of your crazy "get to know Ed" ideas, OK.'

'Don't you want to help me get the boy of my dreams?'

'Sure, just don't expect me to want to nearly die of hypothermia doing it, OK?'

Flora has the sense to look apologetic. She smiles sheepishly at me.

'Sorry, Soph. How about I take you down to the coffee bar to make up for it? Just you and me, best mates. We can have a nice girlie chat over a hot drink, and I promise I won't mention Ed once.'

I'm reluctant to relinquish my spot in front of the fire, but Flora finally persuades me with the promise of a good old gossip and a big squidgy chocolate fudge brownie.

♥

If At First . . .

We've only been in the coffee bar for five minutes when I spot a rather familiar face at the pool table.

I might have guessed Flora had an ulterior motive for dragging me down here!

'Did you *know* Ed was going to be here?' I hiss crossly over the table.

Flora smiles sweetly at me, her face the picture of injured innocence.

'Know?' she repeats. 'How could I know? I just brought my best friend out for a coffee and a brownie to apologise for making her freeze her butt off for nothing, that's all. How was I to know that Ed and his mates come here after every game . . .' She trails off, realising that she's just opened her big mouth and planted both of her size four feet firmly in it. 'I mean, the game was cancelled, wasn't it?' She makes a pathetic attempt to regain some ground. 'You don't want to go, do you . . . ?' she asks reluctantly.

'Just get me that brownie or die very slowly,' I growl at her. Flora's grin is quick to return to her face. She shoots off and returns with two steaming cappuccinos and some slabs of sheer choccy indulgence, but so much for our good old girlie gossip. Sure enough, Flora keeps her promise and doesn't mention Ed once. What she does do, however, is spend the entire time I'm talking to her gazing over my shoulder at him, with a stupid lovesick expression on her face. I could be talking to her in Swahili, naked except for a feather boa and a strategically positioned set of fig leaves and she wouldn't notice. She just sits there and nods or says 'Yeah, me too' every couple of minutes or so, as though this will dupe me into thinking she's actually listening to me, instead of drooling into her coffee cup over sexy Ed.

'Flora!' I splutter, banging my empty coffee cup down on the table.

'What?'

'You're not even listening to me,' I chastise her.

'Of course I am,' she replies without even looking at me. 'Fancy a game of pool? Ed and his mates have just vacated the pool table.'

'No,' I reply sulkily.

'Great!' Flora grins, and heads off to grab a cue.

I sit and mutter maniacally for a few moments, then give in and follow her over. I don't know which is the bigger mug – the one the coffee shop serve their mega-huge hot chocolate with marshmallows in . . . or me.

I chalk my cue, which is the extent of my expertise as far as pool playing goes, and prepare to humiliate myself.

'He's looking over!' Flora shrieks, clutching at my arm in her excitement.

I remove her sharp nails from my soft flesh, and surreptitiously glance over to where Ed and his mates are sitting.

She actually appears to be right. He does seem to be gazing in our direction. He catches me watching him, and hurriedly looks away. He looks really uncomfortable that I caught him looking – that's usually a dead giveaway. Maybe Flora's right, maybe he does like her after all. Either that or he's embarrassed by our terrible pool playing.

It takes us half an hour to get all the balls into the holes, and then only with a marathon amount of cheating, but I've caught Ed looking quite a few times in that long thirty minutes.

'It's no good.' I finally surrender to the inevitable. 'No matter how many times I play this game, I'm still useless. I'm just not cut out to be a pool shark.'

'Well, you've potted a ball more times than I have.' Flora, who wants to keep on playing so that Ed can keep on watching, is far more encouraging than I deserve.

'Yeah . . . but I don't think I'm *supposed* to pot the *white*, am I?'

While I just want to get as far away from the dreaded game as possible, and hide my shame in another cup of cappuccino, Flora's already shovelling more fifty-pence pieces into the pool table.

'Fancy a game of doubles?' she shouts brazenly to Ed. I go crimson, and wonder whether I can follow the cue ball and disappear down the corner pocket.

'Girls versus boys,' Flora suggests.

To my surprise, Ed doesn't tell us to get lost and get a life, but accepts Flora's challenge pretty rapidly, adding further to my gradually growing theory that he's soon to be another in a long line to fall for Flora's very obvious charms.

Flora and I are the most pathetic attempt at a double act ever. We're both worse than useless at the game, and it's not long before we're subjected to a humiliating defeat by Ed and his mate, Sam Rickard.

Flora doesn't seem to care at all though. She's giggling and wiggling round the table, cracking jokes and Olympic-standard flirting. When the game's over she even manages to get Ed and Sam to give her an idiot's guide to playing pool, pretending to be even worse than she actually is so that Ed has to keep on explaining the rudiments to her over and over again.

He's such a nice guy – so kind and patient.

He catches me watching him and Flora, and smiles. 'Would you like me to show you, too?' he asks.

I grin shyly at him.

'No thanks. I think my pool skills are beyond help.'

Besides that, I can't imagine Flora being very happy if I were to drag Ed off for my own private lesson. She's in seventh heaven as, standing behind her, he has to fold his arms around her waist to show her how to place a shot.

Ed and Sam spend the rest of the evening giving us pool lessons. They buy us another coffee, and then at the end of the night they even give us both a lift home. 'See? I told you he wants me,' Flora, grinning broadly, whispers in my ear, as I get out of the car first.

I have to admit I think she's right, but then again Flora normally gets her boy.

I watch them drive off, Flora smiling and flirting like her life depends on it.

It's odd. I'm not really as pleased for her as I should be. I suppose it's because Ed seems like such a nice guy. I wonder if Flora'll do her usual reel 'em in, snog their face off, ship 'em out routine? Bag it, try it, and then on to the next set of lips. Still, you don't play love games with Flora without knowing what you're doing. I guess Ed can take care of himself in the love department.

♥

Peer Pressure

As it's the weekend, I shoot round to Flora's house early the next morning for a news update.

'Well, what happened after you dropped me off?!' I demand, collapsing on the end of Flora's bed.

'He took me home,' Flora replies. She's sitting cross-legged on the floor, scribbling away at a piece of paper.

'That's it?'

She looks up and grins at me. 'Yeah, but it's a good start. He's shy, remember, so he just needs a bit more encouragement . . . and he did ask whether we'd be in the coffee shop again next Friday . . .'

She chews the end of her pen thoughtfully, then waves a piece of paper covered in red felt-tip hearts at me.

'What do you think to this, then? I thought I'd *make* Ed a valentine's card, you know. That way it's more personal, and I'm just trying to think of a poem to put in the middle.'

'What have you got so far?'

'Pool balls are red, cue balls are white, if you've got the balls, then make me yours tonight . . .' Flora giggles, 'and, roses are red, your eyes are blue, give us a snog, or better still two. Or what about, red is the rose, green is the grass, has anyone told you, you've got a cute . . .'

'Flora!' I gape at her in astonishment. 'You can't send those!'

Flora giggles.

'Er . . . look, why don't we just go to the shops and buy one, Flor? Homemade cards are a bit Blue Peter, aren't they?'

'Yeah, maybe you're right.' To my relief, she puts down her pen and screws up the piece of paper she'd been scrawling on. 'Come on, then.'

'Well, I didn't mean like this minute,' I protest, but she's already heading out the door.

There are about eight card shops in the city centre. We manage to go into every single one of them at least three times.

I find some really cute cards, and show Flora one with two hedgehogs cuddling up together on the front.

'How about this, then?'

Flora takes the card from me and looks at it in disgust.

'Crikey, Soph, you can be such a wuss sometimes.

Next you'll be showing me a card with a "cute ickle puppy dog" on the front,' she lisps mockingly.

I surreptitiously slide the one of the baby boxer with a red rose between its teeth back into the rack when she's not looking.

Flora trawls through all the rude or jokey cards before I can finally steer her towards something only semi-embarrassing.

'Aren't you going to get one, then?' she demands as we head for the till.

'And do what . . . send it to my dog?'

'Well he's better looking than some of the boys at college,' Flora jokes. 'No, seriously, I know you always deny it, but there must be someone you fancy?'

'Hardly,' I laugh. 'I think you like the only decent bloke in our year.'

'Yeah,' she grins. 'Ed is lovely isn't he?'

'Yep,' I agree, 'he sure is, but I think I'll leave you to do the "love thang" and give sending a valentine's card a miss this year.'

In the post office, Flora finishes writing something cryptic in her card, adds a dozen kisses, snogs the back of the envelope with a red-lipsticked mouth as she seals it, and then writes 'SWATS' on the back.

'Shouldn't that be SWALK?' I ask her. 'You know, Sealed With A Loving Kiss?'

'Don't be silly, that's pathetic.'

'So what exactly does SWATS stand for?'

'Sealed With A Tonguey Snog!' Flora proclaims with a wicked grin.

I had to ask, didn't I!

She writes out Ed's address, again disguising her spiky scrawl, slaps a stamp on the front, then throws it down the letter chute, sending it on its way with an air kiss.

♥

Uh-Oh

Valentine's Day dawns bright and sunny. I draw back the curtains, and watch as the postman walks out of our front drive and in through next door's gate.

I don't rush downstairs to see what's been delivered. I'm expecting yet another card-free day for me. That is, unless any of my relations have taken pity on me. Last year I got a card from Gran. It wouldn't have been so bad, but she actually signed it 'Love Granny'. How sad can you get?

'Get any valentine's cards, then?' I ask Mum over breakfast.

Dad, who is sitting at the table drinking tea, suddenly looks very guilty, and slopes off to the corner shop saying he's 'just going out to buy a newspaper', which, considering we get one delivered every morning, is pretty suspect.

An impatient, excited Flora is waiting at the end of the road to walk to college with me.

'So d'ya get any cards, then?' she pounces as soon as I get within earshot.

I shake my head.

'Never mind,' she jokes. 'You can have one of mine. I usually get so many the postman has to start weight training in January so that he's got the stamina to carry them all.'

'How many?'

'Well, three actually,' she laughs. 'I'm still trying to work out which one came from Ed . . . Quick, Soph!' Just as we reach the college gates, she stops short and excitedly grabs my arm.

On the other side of the car park, Ed's just getting out of his pride and joy, a dilapidated old Beetle held together by rust and a dodgy purple paint job.

Patience may be a virtue, but it's one Flora's never had. She drags me over and accosts him before he can even lock the rusting door.

'So Ed, has Cupid fired any arrows in your direction yet?'

'You what?'

'It's Valentine's Day isn't it?' she persists. 'Get any cards then?' Ed grins awkwardly. 'Er yeah . . . Actually I got one in the post this morning.'

He shifts uncomfortably from one foot to the other, looking kind of embarrassed. I feel really sorry for him. I can't help thinking how unfair it is of Flora to put him on the spot like this.

'Any ideas who sent you that then?' she beams. 'Obviously a total babe with exceptionally good taste.'

Unless I'm imagining things, she then winks heavily at him. Either that or she's got something stuck in her baby blues. Nope, it was definitely a wink: she's just done it again. She is so embarrassingly unsubtle sometimes! I kick her very quietly on the shin.

'Ouch! Soph!' she hisses.

I glare at her, conveying eyeball messages to give the guy a break, but she refuses to decode my pupils and, briefly glaring back for the kick, ploughs on regardless.

'Well? Who d'ya think sent you the card then, Ed?'

He looks over at me.

He looks back at Flora.

Flora beams encouragingly.

'Well . . . I kinda thought . . . Sophie?'

'Sophie!' Flora splutters. 'Sophie!'

Ed turns to me and smiles shyly. 'Yeah. I was going to come and say thanks. It was . . . like . . . really sweet of you . . .'

'But . . .' I mouth in shock, like a floundering goldfish.

'But!' Flora repeats, like an indignant parrot.

'Maybe . . . I mean, if you're not doing anything tonight,' Ed looks up at me from under long thick brown eyelashes, '. . . perhaps we could meet up at the coffee bar again.'

He's cut short by Flora, eyes blazing with fury, doing a pirouette on the spot, and stomping off.

'Oh dear.' I swivel agitatedly from Ed to Flora, who's doing a major flounce across the car park.

'What's the matter? What's going on, Soph?' Ed puts a warm hand on mine. What a mess, Ed thinks that *I* sent him the card. Flora, my best friend, fancies Ed, and Ed . . . well . . . Ed fancies *me*? What's more, as I look into his beautiful blue-green eyes which are currently swimming with concern, and feel his fingers gently but firmly take a hold of mine, the realisation hits me full in the face with all the force of a hormonal H-bomb, that the feeling might be more than a little bit mutual. Cupid's abandoned his bow and arrows, and is coming straight at me in an unstoppable Sherman tank of emotion.

It's been a while since I did science, but even I can recognise the pure chemistry flowing between us with just that one touch.

I fancy Ed.

I feel like the electricity running between us is lighting up a little neon sign on my forehead, announcing this fact to the world.

Turning bright crimson with a mixture of embarrassment, pleasure and total mortification, I snatch away my hand, and sprint off like a Cinderella whose watch has just hit midnight.

'I'm sorry, I'll try and explain later. Look, I better go after her . . . I'm sorry . . .' Apologising profusely to a very confused-looking Ed, I shoot after my best friend, who has now disappeared into the building

I hunt high and low, but Flora is nowhere to be found. She must be avoiding me. I've got an important class this morning, but I'm too worried about Ed and Flora to listen. My lecturer is merely a constantly moving mouth with no sound.

As soon as the first break hits, I head off to the one place I can almost guarantee to find my absent friend.

It's not the most hygienic place in college, but it's one of the warmest, and it has something that is *definitely* essential to continuing girlie existence – mirrors.

I push open the door to the girls' loo.

'Flora? . . . Flora, it's me, Sophie. Are you there?'

Silence for a moment, and then . . .

'In here,' comes a voice from one of the cubicles.

I expected to hear the suspicious sound of a nose blowing into copious amounts of loo roll, but instead Flora emerges, grins at me in a kind of lopsided sort of fashion, and simply starts to reapply her lip liner.

This must be the calm before the storm.

'Are you OK?' I ask tentatively, waiting for the explosion.

'Sure. Why shouldn't I be?' Flora replies steadily.

I peer closer at her face. She certainly looks OK. I'm totally confused. Maybe this isn't Flora. Maybe the real Flora, the one who buzzed off earlier like an angry wasp, was whisked away by a low-flying UFO and this is an unemotional alien stand-in.

'Well, I thought you'd be upset about . . . you know . . . Ed.' I tack his name to the end of the sentence like it's a taboo word, but Flora doesn't even wince.

'Why on earth should I be upset?' she asks innocently.

'Well . . . you know . . . him thinking I sent him the card, when it came from you . . . and I know how much you like him . . .'

'You don't think that I . . .' she puts a hand to her breast in what I think must be pretend amazement. 'You *do* don't you? You really think that I fancy Ed?' She tries a laugh, but it comes out as a sort of manic-sounding hiccup.

'Well that was kind of the impression you were giving, yeah.' I look at my friend in wide-eyed confusion.

'Oh that . . . well that was the *impression* I wanted to give, but it was actually all part of my cunning plan.' Flora squints into the mirror as she draws black kohl circles around her eyes. 'You see, I knew that he really liked you, and I could guess that you secretly liked him. And because you're so shy and quiet, and he's so shy and quiet, I knew that you two would never get it together if I left you to do it on your own . . .' She's obviously making it up as she goes along, but hey she's my best mate. If a little self-delusion helps her hurt pride, then I'm not going to be the one to burst her bubble.

'So, I sent him the card hoping he'd think it was from you, which he did, so everything's worked, you see. No, the real lucky object of *my* affection is the gorgeous sexy love god who only this morning sent me the most wonderful valentine's card.' She whips a card with a picture of a 'cute wittle puppy dog' on the front, from out of her bag. 'It's from Sam Rickard,' she beams proudly. 'Isn't it sweet?'

'I didn't think you liked cute pup—' I begin.

'Sam's much better looking than Ed, don't you think?' Flora cuts in. 'And he's captain of the rugby team. And he's got a wicked sense of humour ... You know, he can really make me laugh ... Don't you think we make a great couple?'

Well I must admit I'd be more likely to put Flora together with someone like Sam than I would Ed. In fact, now I come to think about it, they're pretty well suited to each other.

'Yeah,' I tell her. 'I think you two'd make an excellent couple.'

'Yeah,' she says, and this time the grin looks pretty genuine. 'So do I ... but what about you and Ed?'

'What *about* me and Ed?'

'Well, he thought you sent him that card.'

'Yeah, I know, but I didn't.'

'Yeees,' Flora says impatiently. 'But he *thought* you did, and he seemed pretty happy about it.'

'Well he wasn't quite chucking his guts, no. But he's probably very self-controlled.'

'Come off it, Soph, he looked totally chuffed . . . You do like him, don't you?'

I nod slowly. The thing is I have always kind of liked Ed, and the more I've got to know him the more I like him, but Flora sort of staked her claim first.

'Well then.' Flora snaps shut her compact, her reflection beaming at me. 'You should just tell him.'

'But I can't do that!'

Flora turns away from the mirror and gives me a hug.

'Look Soph, I know you think I go way over the top occasionally . . .'

'Only occasionally?' I joke.

Flora grins. 'OK, all the time . . . and I know you think that it's the guy's job to do the asking, but sometimes you have to decide what you want and just go for it.'

'But—'

'No, no buts. Ed likes you, you like Ed. It's as simple and as complicated as that. Take a chance for once, Sophie. Remember, nothing ventured . . .'

'And you really wouldn't mind?'

'Mind?' she repeats. 'I got a card from Sam Rickard. Everybody fancies Sam Rickard.'

'Including you?'

'Do I fancy Sam?! Is the food in this place totally inedible? Is spending all of your meagre clothes allowance before the sales total torture? Does my little brother . . . ?'

♥

Sort It Out!

I think about what Flora said all day.

I'm not like her. Call me old-fashioned, but I need the guy to do the asking. I can't think of anything more terrifying than chasing after a guy. You're heading for total humiliation city if it turns out that he's not interested. Then again, Flora seemed pretty sure that he was interested, and he did kind of ask me out tonight . . . I think of the way that he smiled at me earlier, with his eyes as well as his mouth, the gentle touch of his hand on my arm . . .

It's no good. I really do like him. I get this strange sort of feeling in my head and my stomach whenever I think about him. And I've been thinking about him pretty constantly since this morning. I've never been in love before. I get the feeling it's a bit like having flu. I feel hot and then cold, and kind of shaky and light-headed. It's like I've suddenly caught a love bug or something and I'm afraid a little mouth-to-mouth from Ed's lusciously kissable lips is the only cure I can think of.

Oh well – here goes.

Before I can change my mind, I grab the phone – and dial Ed's number.

The phone seems to ring for ever. I'm just about to put it down when Ed answers. I almost chicken out and put the phone down without speaking, but just as I'm reaching for the disconnect button, I think of Ed's cute grin and imagine those lips doing something other than simply smile at me.

Flora's voice echoes through my head: 'Nothing ventured, nothing gained.'

I take a deep breath. 'Hi Ed? Er . . . it's Sophie.'

Half an hour later the doorbell goes.

Within the past thirty minutes I've rapid-changed my way through eight different outfits, reapplied my make-up three times – wavering between red lip-glossed glamour and the bare essentials natural look – and chewed my carefully cultivated nails down to ragged nonexistence. I've tried rehearsing what I'm going to say to him to my reflection in the mirror, but I still haven't got a clue. I'm just going to have to wing it and ad lib! That's if I can actually pluck up the courage to speak to him at all! One final frantic hair and lippy check in the hall mirror, a prayer of thanks that Mum and Dad have gone out and, with madly shaking legs and an idiotically nervous smile, I open the front door.

Ed is standing on the doorstep, huge card in one hand, huge bunch of flowers in the other.

We grin awkwardly at each other.

Now he's actually here, I haven't got a clue what to say to him. There's an agonisingly long silence while I try to get my brain to come up with a reasonably sensible sentence, but all I can do is gaze gooily into his bluey-green eyes.

'Look, about the valentine's card,' we eventually both say together.

We both stop. I laugh nervously.

'You go first,' says Ed.

'No, you first. I insist.'

'Well . . .' he hesitates for a moment, and then, taking a deep breath, plunges in. 'Look, what I was going to say is that I'm really glad you sent me that card, I was going to send you one, but . . . well, basically, I didn't have the guts.' He smiles that slightly lopsided smile of his, the one that I'm starting to like more every time I see it.

'I really like you Soph, I just wasn't sure if you felt the same way . . .' he trails off as he sees my face begin to colour with a faint pink blush.

It's no good, I've got to tell him the truth.

'I didn't send it,' I mumble.

'You what?' He leans forward trying to catch what I'm saying.

'I didn't send you the card, Ed,' I repeat.

'Oh,' he takes a step back and his face kind of freezes in shamed mortification. 'Oh . . . I' he mutters, half-heartedly attempting to shove the bunch of flowers behind his back. He catches his bottom lip with his teeth and chews on it in embarrassment, looking as if he wished the ground would open and swallow him up.

'Oh Ed, I'm really sorry, but . . .' I try to explain.

'No it's OK Sophs, honestly.' He starts to back away.

'I didn't send you the card, Ed . . . but I wish I *had*.' My words come out in a rush, but this time Ed hears me loud and clear.

He stops backing off, drags his eyes up from the pavement, and looks at me hopefully. 'You do?'

'Yep,' I nod slowly.

'But . . . I don't understand . . .'

'I know. Like I said on the phone, I've got some explaining to do . . . Er . . . do you want to come in?'

Ed perches on the sofa slowly drinking coffee, while I start to tell him the whole Flora business – well, nearly the whole Flora business. For the sake of Flora's feelings, I omit the bit about her fancying him, and go for the safer option of the 'Flora-playing-Cupid' story which is her official line now anyway.

I watch his face to see if he's at all mad at being

set up, but that cute smile stays in place the whole time.

'Flora says that sometimes if you really want something then the best thing to do is to just go for it,' I explain.

'Do you think so?' he asks, pushing a stray lock of soft brown hair out of his eyes. I think of all of the hair-brained schemes and trouble Flora's dragged me into over the years through her 'go-get-'em attitude. But if it weren't for her, would I have the cutest guy in the universe sitting only centimetres away from me, gazing at me like *I'm* a gooey chocolate brownie and *he's* hungry?

'I do now,' I laugh happily.

'Well, in that case . . .' Ed puts down his nearly-empty coffee cup, very gently takes my face in his hands and, smiling softly, pulls me to him . . .

Dear Angelo

Sarah Rookledge

Dear Angelo,

It's me, Karis, but then you guessed that from the English stamp. I've got a brand new pad of air-mail paper, I've got your photo smiling up at me through the lipsticky tissues on what passes for my desk and I've got your letter which I read at breakfast time. I guess that makes me to blame for the Rice Krispie stuck to the front!

You asked how things were going with Nat. I thought it was pretty tactful of you not to point out that ever since I started going out with this guy, all I send you is a catalogue of my moans. And to think I was scheming to date him for weeks! Anyway, I'm back on him again today. Dig out my last letter and scribble through the bit where I call him a sleaze bag. I'm feeling guilty already. He *is* all right, I swear, and I have got one choice bit of news (with maybe more to follow).

I took your wise advice and pinned him down about a date. A *real* date, you know. Not hanging around his mate's house. Not watching his band rehearse. You were right when you said I should put him on the spot. 'If we're going out, Nat,' I reasoned, 'how come we never go out?'

I was firm but I was charming (I can be charming, Angelo. I'll give you a demo if we ever meet). You should have seen him. All those little mental cogs began to turn. He made a few swift calculations based on how much money he's got stashed away in that Liquorice Allsorts tin under his bed. Then he suggested we go to this new place that's just opened on the Green. He meant the *Trattoria*. (Who says you never get a word of Italian out of me?) I stayed by the phone while he made the booking and he definitely said 'for two', so unless Reptilian happened to be the cabaret act I'll be free of them for a whole evening. I intend to make the most of it (cue mad witchy cackle). Now I'm off to make my case for Mum's last centimetre of Christmas bubble bath.

Watch this space. I'll finish off tomorrow . . .

Hi I'm back!

What can I say? The bath was pretty hot and steamy. Nothing else was! I was up to my neck in bubbles with my mind on happy things (Nat's sexy eyes, zabaglione for two, those rolled-up Amaretti papers that float up to the ceiling when you burn the ends). Then Mum knocked on the door in this sorry-for-existing sort of way and I just knew the evening wasn't going to go the way I'd planned ...

'Phone for you, Karis.'

I dripped downstairs and said hello. There was a long silence, then Nat's surprised, 'Oh, hi,' as if *I'd* rung *him*, not the other way round.

'Something about tonight?' I prompted.

'Er, yeah. Listen, Karis. I wondered if we could, you know, set another night for it.'

I said nothing. Let him limp on.

'Only Giles is trying to get together a rehearsal for the band. Tonight's the only night everyone's free.' I can't say I was surprised. Brian, Giles, Craigie, Pete or little Tony would not be anyone's idea of a hot date.

'Everyone except *you*, you mean.'

'That's right, unless you and I can . . . reschedule.'

'It was going to be a chance to be just us,' I protested. 'We were going to *talk* to each other.' That seemed to stump him.

'What was it you wanted to say?'

Although a few choice comments came to mind,

none seemed quite withering enough. I opted for the dignity of a stony silence and put down the phone.

So Angelo, where do you reckon I go from here? When I set the whole evening up, I meant it as a test: Hey Nat, I was saying, prove you can put me first. It doesn't seem such a bright idea now it seems I've gone and proved the opposite. It's all very *EXPOSING* (translation – I feel a total prat).

Nat rang up again just before I went to bed. I wouldn't speak to him. Maybe I'm being over-sensitive, it is only one blown date, but I'd be lying if I said there were no hard feelings. What I really fancy doing is staying out of his way for a while. That way he gets the message I'm not always available and I get some time to cool off.

Mum is behaving as if I've got FRAGILE, HANDLE WITH CARE tattooed on my forehead. I'm minding her pottery stall at a craft fair today (no cus-tomers so far, so I'm glad I brought my writing case). I thought I was doing her a favour till I heard her telling Dad that it would 'take my mind off things'. She drove me down in her old van this morning, pointedly Not Mentioning Last Night. (Mostly this meant wittering on about what a mild winter we were having and similar rivetting stuff.) Now she's off to meet a friend. 'An old school friend'

♥ 117 ♥

is how she described this woman to me, which must mean she's known her even longer than I've known you. Blimey.

She's left me all set up for a day's trading. I've got her bum-bag on and her fingerless gloves. The idea of course is that I'm going to spend the whole day having money stuffed at me. All I can say is *fat chance*. I've done a couple of these things for her before and they've always been a total waste of time.

It's pretty boring here on my own, but at least I'm spared the spectacle of Mum looking at her watch every five minutes and saying, 'Well, early days yet!' until it's time to go home.

The nearest I've seen to a genuine punter was a woman with big owl glasses who just went as close as the next stall! The guy there is dead sweet. He's a real festival type, Angelo. He even wears one of those felt jester hats with bells on. (Is that another one of those obscure English references you've been telling me off about? If you're stuck, I'll draw a picture.) I *really* like the little carved fish he makes. Still, business is business, so as soon as she looked up from his stuff for a microsecond I shot her my most welcoming smile to try and lure her over here. I'm either out of practice or else she's a shy type because she scuttled off as far away as she could get. Bit worrying really, particularly since Mr Fish was none too pleased and I'd been hoping to soften him up for a discount.

Tell you what, Angelo, I'll get my mate Megan to take a photo of the kind of smile I gave and you can let me know whether it's scary. I think the last time you saw what my teeth looked like I was still wearing a brace. You're even worse, because until Christmas the only pic I had of you was the one that came with your first ever letter when our teachers set up this whole pen-pal thing. I wonder if anyone else we were at school with is still writing.

Your updated photo caused quite a stir. Everyone I showed it to phwoar-ed and cor-ed a lot (do those words translate?).

Amazingly enough, a customer is giving one of Mum's poppy plates the once-over. I think he's going to ask me a question so I'll close.

Hear from you soon.

Karis.

I tucked my writing case in a box under the stall.
'That one? It's, um, thirty quid. Pounds I mean.' Get a grip, Karis. He didn't flinch or move off. He bought it. After he'd gone I thought I'd spread my

luck around. I got my own purse out and bought two tiny carved green fish for Angelo.

Dear Angelo,

That was a swift reply. I didn't pick the fish because you're a Pisces. Are you trying to hint that you've got a birthday coming up?

You asked me if Nat and me had had a talk about Saturday. Er, not exactly. In fact I've spent most of this week avoiding him. Childish, but who cares when it's *so* satisfying!.

Today is Friday, which meant a 9.30 start at college. I'd just shuddered my way through the first mouthful of machine coffee (convinced that you were drinking some hand-roasted, freshly ground number at the time) when Megan showed up looking much fresher than I felt ...

'Ciao, baby!'

'How did you know I was thinking about Italy?'

Megan swung herself into the seat next to mine. 'It's the way your eyes start looking like these little hard green olives. No, it's cute, honestly.'

'Sounds it. What are you doing in so early? You don't have a class.'

'Dad gave me a lift. What a sweetheart, eh? Forget all the things I said about him.'

'So,' I wondered, 'what will you do now you're here?'

Megan flicked her hair back from her eyes. 'I told Dad I was going to work in the library. I'm all equipped.' She pulled out her Dennis the Menace pencil case and rattled it. 'Or I might get my hair done with *them*. What do you think?'

Two days a week at my college the hairdressing students do cuts for the public. While we nattered, a group of pensioners were patiently waiting for a lift to the sixth floor.

'After all, Karis, it's only two quid and they are *supervised*. I've heard you can even get a perm for seven-fifty.'

'You wouldn't dare. Anyway the trainer only lets in the customers with dodgy eyesight. They don't want law suits on their hands.'

'I could borrow your specs.'

'I need them, I've got a class, remember.' I drained my drink.

'Hang on a minute, Karis. If I see Nat, what should I say? He asked me yesterday if you were laid up with flu or something. When I told him you weren't, he said in that case he must be going out with the Invisible Woman.'

It was true I had carried out my avoidance policy pretty thoroughly. Maybe four days were enough to get the message home.

'I suppose it's only fair to give him a chance to say he's sorry,' I conceded. 'I'll be around at lunch time. You can tell him that . . .' But I could tell she'd tuned out.

'Who's she?' she breathed. 'She's amazing.'

I swivelled round and saw waist-length black hair which swung back as the girl turned her head. Her straight dark eyebrows made her face too fierce to be precisely pretty and she was barely one-fifty centimetres tall. All the same I could see exactly what Megan meant.

'She must be new. If I'd seen her before, I'd remember.'

The afternoon started out pretty well. Nat caught up with me while I was getting lunch. He dived under the barrier by the food counter and squeezed his tray in next to mine. The girl he'd just cut in front of sucked in her breath through her teeth in an outraged whistle, but he pretended not to hear.

'Hi Karis,' he said. He touched my face with his fingertips. His mouth was solemn, with this *tender* smile just waiting at the edges for one of mine to give it permission to spread. Avoiding him hadn't been such a great idea after all. In fact, time apart had had an effect I hadn't banked on. Seeing Nat again, everything that had ever made me fancy him hit me freshly and the shock was like the slap from the wave you didn't see until it drenched you. I tried to look normal, or cooler than normal – not breathless, not impressed.

'Hi,' I said.

When an inconvenient memory of being folded in *those* arms against *those* shoulders threatened to get in the way of my Little Miss Cool, Calm and Collected I fixed my eyes on my tray. Egg, chips, beans and fried mushrooms with chocolate pud to follow should bring me down to earth. Nat followed the direction of my gaze.

'That's the thing about you vegetarians,' he quipped. 'You eat such healthy food.'

As I paid I spotted his mates. AKA Reptilian. They were sprawled across two pushed-together tables. Brian the bassist was making something complicated using everyone else's bendy straws. Giles had improvised a drum with two biros and an upturned polystyrene cup. Warily I eyed the two free spaces up one end (free, that was, if you didn't count the ketchup splodges as having their own place). A discreet distance away was a sunny empty table with two chairs. OK Nat, I thought, let's see if you've learned anything this week. Can it be just you and me sometimes, or do I have to squeeze in with *them*?

'All right, Brian?' he called out, when we reached the bunch of them. 'How're you doing?' but he kept on walking to the small table. He even pulled out my *chair*, which was above and beyond the call, I mean blimey! I plonked myself down. 'Er, ta.'

As we sat there together I remembered all the times I used to stare at him (lech was Megan's word for it) back in September. I'd just started college then and I didn't even know his name. A term later, here we were; a couple (with a few problems, sure, but everyone has those). I could feel the sun on the top of my head. I felt golden. Smug as a cat is how I felt.

Nat was so *nice* it was hard to believe the Saturday phone call ever happened. He didn't even flinch when I popped the yolk of my egg with a big fat chip which Megan always says is totally gross!

'You look gorgeous today, Karis,' he said. I had a washed-out Tweetie Pie T-shirt on and a knackered old pair of jeans . . . but gorgeous? Yes, why not. He looked as if he meant it. This was the way I'd wanted our date to be. Well maybe not the T-shirt and the egg and chips.

'I'm sorry', he said, 'about blowing out the meal and everything. We haven't been out much lately, you're right.'

The moment was so lovely I was tempted to say, 'Oh that's OK, like, mess me around whenever you feel like it,' but I am made of sterner stuff.

'Look, Nat,' I stressed, 'I know your music matters to you but I still need some time when we can be together without the band.'

'I understand that, Karis.' This is easy, I thought. He looked dead sympathetic. He reached across the table and took my hand.

'I've been a jerk,' he mouthed, all penitent. 'This isn't what you deserve.' Damn right it wasn't.

'Thing is, Karis, this is a very important time with my music. There's a lot of stuff up in the air right now. I have to be involved.'

... So there you have it, Angelo. When he said that it was like we'd just driven round a bend in the road together. Now I could see what was waiting up ahead. It looked like the kind of gory accident people brake to gawp at, even though they know they're not going to like what they see.

What came next? Oh yes. Get this. He *explains* to me that everything he does outside his music has to be *dead casual*. This is where he's gone wrong with me, apparently, not realising that!

Hey, I can do casual, I nearly said. Love em and leave em. You ask around. OK, it would have been a dumb thing to say but anyway I never got the chance, cos he'd already shifted up a gear and was speeding right on into 'That's why I think we should end it now.'

Oh Angelo, everything kind of lurched. I could see him thinking, Oh God she's going to cry.

As I bolted for the toilets, Brian — Mr Totally

Crass — leaned over to the table where Nat was still sitting. 'You told her then?' I heard him say. The door out of the canteen wouldn't open. I struggled with it, then realised what the problem was. The girl I'd seen before was tugging from the opposite side. I think I must have given her quite a glare. She dropped the handle like it was on fire.

It was such a horrible way for him to do it, Angelo, in public like that. Even a phone call would have been better. OK, I know that Nat and I hadn't exactly had the perfect relationship but there were some really good bits. I'm sure if he'd been prepared to try we could have made it work.

After I left, all I wanted was to shoot off home and hole up in my bedroom. Thankfully Mum and Dad were both out when I got back. While I had the house to myself I rang Megan. I wasn't in the mood for talking but I didn't want her to get the Chinese whispers version of events that would be everywhere tomorrow. She was sweet. She said just what I wanted to hear which was that, one, Nat was a total loser, and two, that he'd never be lucky enough to get anyone half as nice as me again and when he was an embittered 90-year-old, stashed away in an old folks' home somewhere, he'd be chewing through his zimmer frame in embittered rage at his wasted, loveless life. Suits me.

I hadn't planned on going into college on Monday but she said it was important to show that I was coping. I guess she convinced me cos I gritted my teeth and went. It was awful, though. If I wasn't feeling bad enough already, I learned that the amazing-looking girl both of us saw is actually the latest recruit to Nat's band. No wonder he's been so *busy*. I guess rehearsals have become a pretty attractive proposition.

Megan did a bit of research for me. 'Her name's something like Lucy,' she said, 'only shorter.' Apparently it's Luz. She's Spanish. That seems to make it worse somehow — makes her sort of sexy and exotic. I bet he tells her that he loves her accent. I said as much to Megan and got a telling off: '*Karis*,' she scolded, 'that's not the attitude!' She also warned me about jumping to conclusions. When I said that he hadn't had time for me because he'd been spending it all with Luz she pointed out that I knew nothing for sure. Well admittedly it's not exactly evidence, but it's pretty damn suspicious, don't you think?

Dear Karis,

I was so sad for you when I got your last letter. I know you will not believe me when I say this, but I must tell you that the pain of these things does not last.

In my letters to you last year I often mention a girl called Mercedes. She has red hairs, I write and you say, 'Hair, Angelo: in English it's "hair".' Maybe you remember that? Anyway I write about Mercedes and then I don't because I think if I explain it will make me sad. What happens is her family find another house. I look at the map and think it isn't too far. I can visit, I have my scooter. A few times, that is what we do. Then she writes and says it is no good, now she has other friends, it isn't the same. So I go down to where she lives and I don't even go in to see her. I sit outside her house for a while. I think, she is with someone else now, but I don't want to know for sure. All the time I am thinking, if I had done this thing, that thing, you know?

'Lets have a look, Karis!'

I should have known it was a mistake to try and read Angelo's letter on the bus.

'Oi!' I squealed. 'Paws off.' But Megan shamelessly snatched it from me. Angelo's handwriting was my next line of defence. She squinted down at it, trying to home in on a recognisable word.

'He's got a Mercedes?!' She struggled on. 'Oh, she's his girlfriend.'

'Ex-girlfriend actually.' I realised guiltily that when

her name stopped appearing in Angelo's letters I had never asked him why. 'Give it here, can you!'

Ignoring me, she carried on scanning, 'Ex-girlfriend, yeah. Blah blah blah. Oh, he says he saw her again this Christmas. Didn't feel anything, not a flicker. In fact he thinks he's well out of it now. Reckons in a while it will be like that for you with Nat.'

'*Megan*, that is my private letter. Can I read it for myself?'

'In a minute. He doesn't reckon Nat is seeing Luz – at least, she might not be. *See*, that's what I think too. Hey, let me read you this bit: "It makes me laugh that you are jealous that she's Spanish. Exotic you say, more sexy because foreign, but for me of course you are foreign as her. Is Italian sexy? I should like to know." Hmm, bit of a leading question, that.'

Dear Angelo,

What am I going to do with Megan? We went shopping for valentine's cards today, although it's still ages away. She embarrassed the hell out of me. What's worse, she enjoyed it. We were in this posh shop when she pushed a card into my hand . . .

'Here,' she said, 'What do you think of this one then?'

I peeped inside, then quickly put it back on the rack.

'The look on your face, Karis! I didn't know you were so easily shocked.'

'You'd be surprised. Anyway, isn't there a law about sending obscene material through the post?'

'If it was obscene, it wouldn't be in a shop, would it?' Megan reasoned. 'Well, not one like THIS.'

I had to admit she had a point. The place was *extremely* smart. The man in charge looked like he was fighting off the urge to ask us to wash our hands before we touched any more of his stock. Hanging on strings across the window was a display of perspex jewellery which I wanted instantly. The sun shining through it made coloured shadows on the white walls the way you get in a church.

'Who were you thinking of sending it to?' I asked her.

'I don't know, do I? I just buy the ones I like and figure that out later. I always spend *loads* at Valentine's Day.' This last bit was loud for the benefit of said man who looked about to muscle in with one of those chilly can-I-help-you numbers. 'Anyway, it's only a giggle isn't it, Karis? People don't take it seriously.'

Speak for yourself, I thought. Before we left, Megan threw up her arms and leaned against the wall, doing her best impression of a smouldering pout.

'You can *search* us, you know. If you're worried.'

He sensibly pretended he hadn't heard her and acted very busy on the mirrors with a can of Windolene.

'Megan!' I wailed when we were out of earshot.

'He deserved it. I don't like being made to feel *uncomfortable*. I am the customer after all.'

After that I bowed out of the hunt and left her trekking off to Woollies, ready to sink her quids in a selection box of twenty assorted, if one could be tracked down.

'It's how I bought my Christmas cards,' she said sniffily when I ridiculed the plan. 'All I can say is, if they don't do them, they should.' She flicked back her hair Miss Piggy fashion and strode off up the street . . .

. . . After she'd gone I wondered if she was on to something. What do you think, Angelo? Is Megan just some weird soul with an overactive sex drive? No, don't answer that. What I really mean is, are there enough people like her out there to make a bit of dosh out of? Maybe I'm letting you in on a great marketing opportunity.

It makes me wonder what kind of valentines you'd need to put *in* a box like that. Some cheap and cheerful stuff, of course, like Megan always sends out to her mates, and one huge slushy one — in silver I reckon — with a red rose or a fluffy bunny for the steady.

Then something blush-inducing and definitely anonymous for the object of your lust. Whoever it is you've been staring at slack-jawed at every party while your best mate tries to tell you the taco chip you think you're eating is really a piece of your polystyrene cup (or is it only me that happens to?).

What would be in there for Nat, Angelo? For someone I love who's just told me it's over? I start feeling low and then begin thinking. Did he buy me a card before we split or did he look at the displays and say, '14th February? I won't still be with her by then'? Or maybe he bought me one and now Luz will get it. Kind of waste not, want not. He wouldn't do that, would he? That'd be the worst, if she got something from him that was meant for me.

Should I include an anti-valentine? Something tasteful. Myself, I'd go for a design of reptiles: a venomous snake or two, a poisonous toad ...

Yours maliciously

Karis

'Anything about me in there?' a voice whispered. I zipped up my writing case pronto. 'Er, hi Megan.' I wasn't sure how long she'd been in the library.

'Just the odd mention here and there. Angelo always likes to hear how you're doing.'

She slid up on to the shiny top of the library desk, pushing my files aside to make a space.

'I suppose that's natural. Still, you shouldn't be writing to him, you skiver. Urgent essay – that was your excuse when you disappeared up here. Repeal of the Corn Laws, wasn't it?' She picked up my textbook and flicked through pages of tiny black print. 'Doesn't look too exciting I must say.'

'I did do a bit!' I defended myself. 'I'm just taking a break.'

'I was only teasing. I think you're doing brilliantly.' She reached round me and squeezed my shoulders. 'You are all right now, Karis? Things going OK?'

'Kind of. If I see Nat I feel funny. Otherwise I'm fine.' I squared my shoulders. 'Oh Angelo's probably right. Give it a while and I won't know what I saw in the guy.'

'Right,' said Megan but I don't think I convinced her. I hadn't convinced myself.

'If you two want to talk,' the librarian hissed at us, 'I suggest you go outside.'

I settled my specs on my nose.

'I think I ought to get another hour in, Megan. Then we can go and get a coffee or something.

'Another hour!' she wailed. 'It's six o'clock already.'

I looked at my watch, then down at my notepad.

Great doodles, not so sure about the nineteen different opening sentences, especially since they were as far as I'd got. 'I guess I'll be fresher in the morning,' I sighed.

'Bound to be,' said Megan perkily.

We both sloped out and took the lift downstairs. 'Look,' she said when the doors hissed open, 'the night shift's on.'

I looked around. 'What a lot of suits!'

'The thought of it tires me out,' Megan shuddered. 'Imagine working all day and then coming here to do accountancy or something.'

I felt in my pocket and found three pound coins. 'I'm sure it has its advantages. I bet they're not skint, for a start. Do you want to stay here? I think I've got enough for a coffee and a flapjack at that place by the bridge.'

Megan considered it. 'Sounds OK.'

I put on my jacket to go, then I heard something that stopped me. Music. The canteen is an L shape and the part I couldn't see has a big room opening out from it that's used for gigs and shows, stuff like that. The tune was familiar, and it made me *curious*. I began to move towards the source of it. Megan put her hand on my arm, 'Are you sure?'

'Yes,' I snapped. 'Coming too?'

Dear Angelo,

I am a prize one wally. I am a total dork. What's more, I'm *thrilled* to be one. Apparently Nat and Luz aren't your average loving couple after all. I've obviously been way off the mark about them from the start.

While I was thinking Nat had been lured away from me by Luz's smouldering Spanish eyes, all she ever had her peepers on was his job!

I don't know how long it would have taken me to figure this out on my own, but as things turned out I haven't had to. Yesterday Megan and I were walking past the hall and the band were playing. I couldn't resist it, Angelo. I know they're nothing to do with me any more but I just couldn't miss the chance to have one last look.

I heard Luz before I saw her. Her voice lifted up above the clatter of plates and the hiss of the coffee machine. The song was definitely one of Nat's. I'd been there the afternoon he wrote it. I remembered him scribbling a line, singing it, changing it round, scribbling again in his cramped black writing. In Luz's version Nat's thrashy, crashy sound had softened into something more ballady, but she had a roughness in her voice that gave it edge.

I was hoping I could see and not be seen, and luckily

there were enough people watching for me and Megan to slide in and find ourselves tucked-away places at one side of the room. Luz wore the black leather trousers she'd had on every time I'd seen her, plus a white shirt that made her look like a pint-sized buccaneer.

'Good grief! Fancies herself, doesn't she?' said Megan scornfully. She was being loyal but not exactly fair. I thought Luz sang as if she hadn't noticed everyone was watching her or else she didn't care. She could have been alone in her bedroom from the relaxed expression on her face.

'Turned out from the warm, I'm kicking up a storm,' she sang and I watched her fingers move up and down her guitar. I knew Megan's attention was fixed on me not the band. How was I taking it? What would I do? I'm sure she was also wondering the same thing I was: Where was Nat?

If she wanted a reaction out of me she didn't get it.

'Not bad,' I said, coolly. 'It's a great voice, and she is "*eye-catching*".' It didn't need saying. Brian and Giles, Pete, Craigie, little Tony were all playing better than I would have believed, but it was obviously Luz who had gathered the crowd. Lots of the suits had brought their coffees in. Still holding cups, they twitched and foot-tapped up at the front. There were daytime students in the audience too. Every pair of eyes seemed hypnotised by that ink-black sheet of hair, that purple pout. How could I compete with that? A swimmy jealous feeling stirred inside me, and then a much more concrete pain.

'Ouch!' I squeaked out as Megan jabbed me with her elbow. 'What did you do that for?' I spun round scowling. And then I saw *why* she'd had to make me take notice. Nat had found himself a vantage point even more obscure than ours. He lurked behind a pillar watching Luz sing his song. Was he proud? Was he beaming? Was he hell!

'Maybe they've had a bit of a row,' volunteered Megan.

'Maybe she's murdered his mother and burned down his house,' I said.

So Angelo, what do you think of that? When you and Megan told me I was jumping to conclusions before, I thought you were just being kind (well, kind or *dumb*, frankly). Forgive me. I watched him glower at her through a couple of numbers then I slipped out of the room and went off feeling buzzy and light-headed. I feel sad still but I don't feel jealous — and believe me it's a huge improvement.

Life is weirder than I thought.

Karis

The last of the gaps in the Nat and Luz story got filled in next morning when I ran into Giles. Giles is the band's drummer and, according to Nat, a great laugh. Unfortunately he's also terminally shy with anyone female. In the circumstances I expected him to nod hello and make tracks, but when I dived into the eight-till-late to get some milk for breakfast he followed. He was hovering beside me when I hefted a four-pint of semi-skimmed out of the fridge.

'I saw you play last night,' I said to break the silence.

He blushed, as I knew he would.

'It was OK, wasn't it?' he managed. 'I mean, people clapped and stuff.'

His eyes scanned the shelves. He grabbed a packet of chocolate Hobnobs and another of custard creams. Maybe he's just *shopping*, Karis, I thought. But then he blurted out, 'Have you heard from Nat?' It wasn't exactly a tactful question in the circumstances.

'I'm not likely to, am I? We've split.'

'Yeah, I know.' He went redder still – if that was possible.

'I thought you'd have seen him yourself. He was there last night.'

This was obviously news to Giles who visibly winced. 'I noticed he wasn't playing,' I said.

Giles nerved himself to spell out the brutal truth.

'Nat isn't with the band any more, Karis. He quit

when Luz took over from him as lead vocalist. It was a hard decision for all of us. Things got pretty heavy.'

This didn't surprise me. I could imagine Nat's reaction to a coup.

'We had a secret ballot in the end. I didn't vote for her, of course, but it was the *majority decision*.' Giles looked wistful. 'She does have an *amazing* voice, Karis, and since she joined we've got a load of gigs lined up.' He dragged a crumpled flyer for a local music pub from the back pocket of his jeans and smoothed it out. He looked proud and shamefaced at the same time. They'd been disloyal, but a gig was a gig.

'See, this is us, the support. It's on next Saturday.' The blush rushed back. 'Come if you can.'

'I'm tied up Saturday,' I fibbed, 'but thanks for the offer.' I paid for my milk.

'See you, Giles.' When I turned to go, his expression stopped me.

'I'm worried about him, Karis. He hasn't spoken to me since. If you do see him tell him to give me a call.'

'Give him time, he's probably feeling hurt.' I hadn't expected to find myself in the lofty position of feeling sorry for Nat. I was about to head home but there was something I needed to clear up.

'Before Nat and Luz fell out over who was going to sing, she wasn't ever, you know, *seeing him*, was she?'

'Not if he saw her first.' Giles bayed with laughter at his own bad joke. 'Karis, you didn't think . . . ?'

It was my turn to blush. 'I did wonder.'

'She's not his type and I don't think he's hers. Apart from that . . . well he *hates* her, Karis. He always has.'

Dear Angelo,

I'm over him! It's true. I feel *so* positive. I hope *you* believe me cos Megan's acting sceptical. Oh, she made all the right noises when I told her the good news but I could see she had her doubts. When I probed a bit she admitted she thought it was too soon. She's been brilliant all the time I've been down and I guess it's sweet that she fusses, but I don't think she's grasped that everything's changed.

OK, I grant you Nat *did* chuck me and it was an evil thing to do. But it wasn't personal, was it? He just knew the band had this plot to squeeze him out and he didn't trust them alone for a minute, even to spend time with me. Besides, I've been revenged without having to lift a finger.

I tell you Angelo, I'm really buzzing. I went out running today for the first time in weeks (and don't remind me running was my New Year's resolution!) I'm sure a *nice* girl would be really sympathetic about poor old Nat's attack by ruthless Luz but I'm not that girl. At least not yet. Give me a month and I might mellow.

Your indestructible friend

Karis

'What d'you reckon that is, then?' It was February 7th and I was sitting in Megan's bedroom. Just below the message on the card she passed me was a red blob of something waxy. I scratched it with my fingernail and sniffed the bit that came off.

'Dunno. Lipstick?

'*Of course* it's lipstick, duh-brain. What I'm asking you is, can you tell how I made the mark?'

Nothing came to mind. She took the valentine back off me, held it out at arm's length and wrinkled her nose.

'It doesn't really work, does it?' she eventually conceded. 'And you can't get two on because the card's not big enough.' She scraped up a lipstick from the top of her dressing table, drew her lips taut over her teeth and began to paint. When she'd got her mouth the way she liked it she took a clean card off the pile and puckered up. 'Back to the tried and tested. There, that's not bad.'

I looked down at the perfect cupid's bow she'd made, then at the first card with the blob.

'Megan, it's not, you know, your *nipple*, is it?'

She threw back her head and laughed. 'That'd be telling.' She added the new card to the pile. 'There, I think I've done them all. Unless I meet a total hunk in the next week, that is. Are you sending any?'

'I haven't got anyone to send one to.'

'I don't have a boyfriend but that doesn't stop me. What about *Angelo*?'

'That's a purely platonic thing, Megan.'

She looked at me a bit too closely. I squirmed away and wouldn't meet her eye. 'Well, I have known him since I was eight. We're like . . .'

'Brother and sister?'

'Maybe cousins.'

'Which is why you keep his photo in your purse.'

'Megan! I just put it there one day and forgot to take it out.'

'Of course, easily done.'

She tidied her cards and address book and put them on the shelf above her desk. I thought she'd finished teasing me but she hadn't quite.

'How about a platonic valentine? I'll write you something. What d'you reckon on this: "Roses are red, violets are blue, I swear I'll keep my hands off you"?'

'Not too difficult,' I laughed, 'seeing as Angelo and I aren't even in the same country.'

Megan sat down on the edge of the bed and swung

her feet. Ten varnished nails winked as they caught the light.

'What's the problem, Karis? Worried you'll scare him off?'

'Well I wouldn't want to risk it. He's really important to me, Megan. He gives me loads of good advice and he's always there for me. Friends like that are hard to find.'

'Thank you Miss Tactful.'

'I didn't mean—'

'I should hope not. Come on, I made a load of popcorn earlier. If we go down to the kitchen now we can scoff it all before my brother gets back.'

Walking home from Megan's I had to pass the house where I'd first got it together with Nat. We'd both turned up at the same party. Although it was the first time we'd spoken, I think all those longing glances I'd been shooting him at college must have made an impression because he walked up to me while I was still taking my coat off. 'I know I know you,' he said, 'I just don't know your name.' It had been an evening glimpsed in snapshots – tiny surfacings from Nat's long kiss.

I felt inside my pockets and pulled my gloves on. The party night had been cold like this one, but so hot indoors everyone had run round throwing windows open. Music and voices had spilled out on to the lawn. Tonight, as I watched the house, a woman drew the curtains. She did each room in turn, closing off the cosy yellow blocks of light. I was on the outside this time and that was just how I felt. Outside and alone.

So I was over Nat, was I? Maybe I was but I certainly missed that feeling he used to give me. It hadn't all been bad. There were some pretty romantic times too. After the party he'd walked me back home along this road. I could remember his jacket against my cheek, and his special smell. The next time we'd met he had a song to show me. 'I went straight home', he said 'and I wrote this about you.'

What I want to know is, why does this kind of memory pop into your head when you least need it? When I got back to my house I hid myself away in my room. With wet hair combed down either side of my face I looked as doleful as I felt.

Poor Karis, I thought, life's not fair, is it? I took out my writing case and scribbled down one of the shortest letters Angelo had ever had from me.

Dear Angelo,

There's a week to go till Valentine's Day and I wish that I could have it cancelled. I don't *want* to go downstairs to an empty doormat and my parents' sympathetic glances. Nobody loves me, Angelo. It's not fair. I want to be the first choice of someone gorgeous. I don't care if that's a stupid thing to say – it's true.

Is there any hope for me?

Karis

I put the cap back on my biro, tucked the letter in an envelope and stuck on the stamp. Heavy rain had started up. Car-wash sounds swooshed beyond the curtains. If it wasn't for that, I'd have gone out to post it straight away.

Then Dad knocked at the bedroom door.

'You missed supper. Did you eat at Megan's?'

'Not a proper meal.'

'We kept you back some pasta. It's a bit congealed but I can heat it up if you like.'

'Sounds stunning. Go on then, I'll risk it.' Neither of my parents are great cooks but I still felt more cheerful once I'd eaten and ashamed of writing such a whinge. Poor Angelo. He'd had moan, moan, moan from me lately. And he was always so nice in return. I really didn't deserve him. I nearly binned the letter straight away but it had my last stamp on. In the morning I would soak it off.

I dimly remember Dad bringing in my tea but I

burrowed deeper into my duvet. I was having a dream that owed a lot to me and Megan going to see *Il Postino*. A dark-haired postman on an ancient bike was slowly spiralling up a dusty yellow hill. Luz and Angelo watched him coming from outside the house on the top. They were sitting at a table sharing a bunch of black grapes . . .

'Karis!' It was Mum's voice this time. I opened my eyes. The tea on the bedside table was stone cold and there was a space beside it where last night there had been an envelope.

I grabbed my kimono thingy off the hook on the back of the door and knotted the belt as I stumbled downstairs.

'Where's my letter, Mum?'

She stood in the hall sipping sugarless coffee (she was trying to give up).

'Your dad took it with him when he went to work. He had a couple of his own to go. Thought he'd save you the trouble.'

'How long since he left?' I considered tearing up the street in my dressing gown.

Mum looked at her watch. 'About a quarter of an hour ago. He did *tell* you he was taking it. He thought you heard him. You gave a kind of groan.'

Angelo will write back, I thought, and then I'll stop worrying. It never takes him long.

*

Well I waited. Nothing came. 'It's been ages,' I fretted and, though Megan pointed out it wasn't ages but just a few days, it didn't make me feel better. It was a long time for *him* and I knew the reason why. Who could blame Angelo for not writing back when I was such a miserable cow? I tried to write to him again but everything came out wrong. I couldn't understand why it was so hard. I'd never had any trouble finding what to say before but now it seemed really important, like every word had a hidden meaning. I wanted to get it right because I realised suddenly how much Angelo meant to me, and I might never hear from him again . . .

'See,' said Mum, 'I knew you'd get one.' She had propped the envelope behind my cereal bowl where I spotted it when I went down to make a coffee.

'You've been walking round all week with your bottom lip stuck out like a dinner plate and all the time I was sure there'd be something. A lovely girl like you.'

'Yeah, well maybe you're partial.' I swung my college bag on to my back. 'Actually I wasn't planning on breakfast today, Mum,' I said primly. 'I've got a lecture first thing and then an essay with a long list of background reading.'

'But you must open your card, Karis. I'm sure I know that writing. I just can't quite place—'

I could place it. I saw it every day.

'I'll look at it later.' I saw her face fall. She was so sure this card was going to be just the thing to turn my mood around and she wanted to be there to see it.

'Oh, go on then,' I groaned, 'give it here.'

I opened it in silence then handed it to her.

'Have a look if you like, Mum, it's nothing private.'

She hesitated but she took it. 'A bunch of gladioli and a kitten. How nice. And what's this inside, Karis? This red splodge . . . ?'

'Couldn't tell you, Mum, I'm sure.'

It was just after eight when I headed for the bus stop. The light of the last few streetlamps coloured the puddles. The drawstring hood of the postman's kagoule reduced his face to a tiny oval, like a person drawn on a spoon. From the way he slammed the gates I didn't think he reckoned much on Valentine's Day either.

'Not a very good likeness is it, love?' the bus driver quipped, peering at the smiling photo on my pass. I curled my lip at him and stomped off to the back. Not only had I lost my boyfriend I'd gone and lost my best friend in the whole world – Angelo. And it was all my own fault. I'd got nothing and I deserved nothing. As if to demonstrate the day had it in for me, the bus broke down. I had to wait and swap on to another. When I pushed into my usual classroom late, the blinds were drawn. A woman I didn't know was whizzing through slides on a carousel projector. She squeezed a button and a pillared building changed to a head in profile. 'Lorenzo the Magnificent,' she proclaimed, 'by Botticelli.' It wasn't Angelo exactly, but it could have been a cousin of his.

'*Buongiorno*?' The keeper of the button swivelled an icy eye towards the crack of light which I had foolishly dared to make by standing in the doorway. Someone in the back row said helpfully, 'Your lot are downstairs today,' but I didn't fancy hunting them out. I headed for the library, kidding myself I was going to do some work, but really after somewhere quiet to brood. There were only two other students in there. Unfortunately they were playing eye-games with each other over their books. After half an hour of witnessing coy little smiles and quick glances away, my mood was even more murderous. This was the most miserable day of my life and here they were insensitively flirting! I scowled at them a while, not doing my essay, then I caught another bus back home.

The letter must have come second post. It was on the mat when I opened the door. *His* writing of my name. *His* stamp. The hall smells nice, I remember thinking.

I found out why when I carried the letter off to read in the living room. When I pushed the door open I got the full scent of the flowers. They were still in their cellophane, complete with satin bow, but Mum, ever practical, had stuck the ends into the heavy jug that always stood in the fireplace. A note in her writing said, 'These came after you left!!!' Another on a florist's card said, 'Karis, *ti' amo*, my beautiful Valentine.' I sat down next to them and read.

Dear Karis,

I am sending flowers. I do not know what flowers you like so I say in the shop give her what smells best and is most beautiful. I hope they are how you want.

They are, I wanted to say, looking at soft-headed roses in a dusky pink, scented lilies, little stars of jasmine (at *this* time of year!), a mist of green.

Karis, the letter you are reading is one I have written many times and not sent. I wish the letter was as easy as the flowers, because if I write and say 'Karis I love you', it may be too soon because you are missing Nat still and if I wait, well maybe there will be someone else and I will miss my luck.

Also I am in Italy, which you will think is too far away to have a boyfriend.

Today I looked at your letter again. You say no one loves you and I am here reading it and I know that I anyway love you. I think, even if I am not the perfect person, even if I'm just a friend to you and anyway a friend far away, it is better to say this than not say and wonder. Also today I have some news.

Karis, my parents are coming to England for two weeks in one month's time and I am coming too. So, for a while anyway, we will be close enough to meet. Is that what you would like? Write and tell me. When we fly I will phone.

When I'd finished reading I could feel my face had stuck in a crazy grin. All those letters, I was thinking, eight years of letters but I've never had to write a love letter until now. In a little while I'd go and fetch my writing case, but right now called for something more immediate. I took his photo from my purse and kissed it. '*Dear* Angelo,' I said.

J·17

Subscribe now!

Get your fave mag delivered to your door every blimmin' month for a year and never miss a copy! How? Simply complete your details and return this coupon with your payment to *J17* Subscriptions Department, Tower House, Sovereign Park, Market Harborough, Leicestershire LE16 9EF.

☐ I enclose a cheque/postal order made payable to *J17* magazine for £19.20 (UK rate)

Please debit my Access/Visa/Amex/Diners

☐☐☐☐☐☐☐☐☐☐☐☐☐☐☐☐

Expiry date_____ Signature _____

Date_____

Name _____

Address_____

_____ Postcode _____

Or phone the Subscriptions Orders Hotline
01858 435339
Between 9.30am and 5.30pm Monday to Friday

Source code WA 1A
Offer code A12